THE BOOK ₒf US

ALSO BY SHANE PEACOCK

Unusual Heroes (2002)
The Artist and Me (2016)

Dylan Maples Adventures
Monster in the Mountains (2003)
Phantom of Fire (2019)

The Dark Missions of Edgar Brim Trilogy
The Dark Missions of Edgar Brim (2016)
Monster (2018)
Demon (2019)

Seven series
Last Message (2012)
Double You (2014)
Separated (2016)

The Boy Sherlock Holmes series
Eye of the Crow (2007)
Death in the Air (2008)
Vanishing Girl (2009)
The Secret Fiend (2010)
The Dragon Turn (2011)
Becoming Holmes (2014)

SHANE PEACOCK

DCB

The publisher gratefully acknowledges the support of the Canada Council
for the Arts and the Ontario Arts Council for its publishing program.
We acknowledge the financial support of the Government of Canada through
the Canada Book Fund (CBF) for our publishing activities, and the
Government of Ontario through Ontario Creates, an agency of the Ontario
Ministry of Culture, and the Ontario Book Publishing Tax Credit Program.

LIBRARY AND ARCHIVES CANADA CATALOGUING IN PUBLICATION

Title: The book of us / Shane Peacock.
Names: Peacock, Shane, author.
Identifiers: Canadiana (print) 20220218269 | Canadiana (ebook) 20220218277 |
ISBN 9781770866553 (softcover) | ISBN 9781770866560 (HTML)
Classification: LCC PS8581.E234 B67 2022 | DDC JC813/.54—dc23

United States Library of Congress Control Number: 9781770866553

Cover art: Nick Craine
Interior text design: Tannice Goddard / tannicegdesigns.ca

Manufactured by Houghton Boston in Saskatoon, Saskatchewan in August, 2022.

Printed using paper from a responsible and sustainable resource,
including a mix of virgin fibres and recycled materials.

Printed and bound in Canada.

DCB Young Readers
An imprint of Cormorant Books Inc.
260 SPADINA AVENUE, SUITE 502, TORONTO, ONTARIO, M5T 2E4
www.dcbyoungreaders.com
www.cormorantbooks.com

"Everybody worships.
The only choice we get is what to worship."

This Is Water

For Miranda,
who was everything to me.

Prologue

THE TRUTH IS, I am writing this to impress you.

Maybe all novels are like that.

This is my gift to you: a story about two people who are no longer together, because one of them made a big mistake. He will not give her up, though — not ever.

What follows is what really happened,[1] right up until the ending, which is a mystery to me. You will create that part ... and I will add it as the last chapter.

---

1 I had to make up a few minor things, though, since this is, after all, a novel.

1
Big Mistake

LATE IN THE SUMMER, late in the afternoon, late in the game that it seemed he was surely going to win, Noah Greene destroyed everything. It only happened because he was certain that Miranda wasn't there. No, that isn't strictly true. It was actually because of other things, things inside him, not just in his head or his heart but deeper, in his soul.

From the interior of the little portable change room, plastic and hot, he could hear the waves breaking against the shore, the seagulls and children shrieking, and the dull hum of adult conversation, but they were all just distant noises pinging around in another world, an outside reality. He could hear Rosie and Walker, Constance and Bruce, no more than the flip of a Frisbee away, but it was the irresistible words of the young woman who was in there with him that were real. They were penetrating his brain.

"I like you, you know, a lot."

Everyone wanted Lisa Ann Bordeaux. All the guys, that is, or at least most of the guys — the guys who liked girls; and some of the girls wanted her too — the girls who liked girls. It was said she would do things that not many others would do, but not with just anybody. Brown eyes, shaggy blond hair, discriminating in the right way. She was cool. Amazing one-on-one, when she decided you were it.[2]

Noah was it that day.

Ten minutes earlier, he had not even known Lisa Ann was there, anywhere on the beach. It was only supposed to be the six of them.

"Where's Mir?" asked Constance.

Back in those days, Noah always thought her haircut should be short and severe. It was long, though, and luxurious, hanging down past her shoulders in shining black ringlets, a perfect contrast with what she called her "white colonial skin." He also thought the fact that Constance wore makeup didn't fit, but she did, lots of it.

"She said she'd be here at six," said Noah.

"5:33:33," said Bruce, head down at his phone, lisping through his retainer. "Thirty-three minutes and thirty-three seconds after five o'clock, August 27, in the year of Anno Dom —"

"We get it, Brew," said Walker. "She'll be here in a bit less than half."

"She can get here whenever she wants," said Constance.

---

2   I don't mean to objectify Lisa Ann in any way. I hope this doesn't. I'm just saying what everyone saw, you know, from the outside.

"You guys can't tell her what to do." She looked at Noah. "'Boyfriend' doesn't mean 'master.'"

Walker frowned and shrugged his shoulders.

"Uh, not saying any of that, Connie."

"Constance! Stop calling me that ... Walkie!"

They spread their beach towels out on the sand. Rosie had a hamper full of food. She had volunteered to bring the whole dinner.

"I made some of your favorites, Noah."

He could never figure out how she knew what he liked. He must have let it slip some time and she had memorized it, seized on it like the combination for her lock.

Rosie set the butter tarts out first, laying them down on her big blue towel beside what she called her "stumpy legs," which were bulging as she knelt to unload the hamper. She wore her cut-offs long, nearly halfway down her thighs.

. "Thanks," said Noah, looking away from her for a change room. He tossed his backpack down and dug around in it. "Forgot to wear my swimsuit underneath."

Bruce had worn his to the beach. It was a loud, stars-and-stripes item at least a size and an era too snug, and he hadn't bothered to wear pants over top. His body was ninety-nine percent dark skin and one percent swimsuit. But the others were just now wriggling out of their clothes. Walker Jones was standing to take down his jeans and reveal his knee-length, one-color orange Nike-swooped suit that he had carefully chosen at the best store for the beach in town. Constance lay down and emerged out of her black track pants in her gray one-piece, pulling it down at the crotch and the back to make sure nothing was exposed. Noah stood up and looked around. The portable change rooms were bright blue and spaced on the beach about a hundred strides apart, all unisex.

Rosie soon had all the food out and stood up too, the shortest of the group. She looked around. Noah was maybe three feet from her. She could reach out and touch him. She pulled off her tee, doing that thing the attractive girls do when they cross their arms at the front and pull upward. Rosie didn't count herself as attractive, so it felt like an act. She didn't have the balls to shake her hair when she unveiled her suit top. There wasn't much to her hair anyway, dark brown and in a pony-tail. Her eyes caught Noah looking around. He wasn't noticing her. She took off her jeans, wondering if he'd see that, sliding them down with a wiggle, but not bold enough to turn around to do it, butt to the fore.

"Are you sure you want that one?" Rosie's mother had asked her when she'd purchased her swimsuit a few months ago. "It's kind of small."

"And kind of red," said her little sister. "It will look like a light on the beach, beckoning the boys."

Rosie had rolled her eyes at her, but she'd bought the suit. It actually wasn't very revealing, not that she thought she had a lot to reveal. It was just that it wasn't quite her style. Whatever her style was. She promised herself she wouldn't be self-conscious in it, but she was, the instant she was exposed. That was how she felt. Exposed.[3]

---

3   Rosie told me all this: about what she was thinking, her swimsuit, even the boy's torsos thing that comes later, turned red when she did. I am not pretending I know what goes on in a girl's head.

Noah was turned the other way. He'd spotted the closest change room and from where he was standing could tell that it was unoccupied, the image of the green traffic light evident in the handle you slid across once you were inside.

Rosie could feel Walker's eyes on her, and Bruce's too. She wasn't sure if their attention[4] was a compliment or not. Boys got weird about bikinis. You would think they'd never seen a girl in the flesh before, or at least in a lot of flesh. Noah wasn't weird about it, at least, not about her standing there in one, exposed. That was understandable, though. He had Miranda. Just months ago, it was all different. He hadn't seemed like he was in her league. But then, what boy is, really? Rosie had known something most girls didn't, though. Noah Greene had always been in Miranda's league. He was in all of their leagues. She could have told anyone that.

"I'm gonna change," he said, walking toward the blue cubicle in the hot sand with his bathing suit in hand, which Rosie had known was loose-fitting but tight in the right places, perfect on him ... and red. He didn't turn back to her at all when he said it, didn't turn his brown eyes on her or sweep back his longish, light brown hair the way he always did when he looked at you and started a conversation. He did pull off his shirt, though, as he walked. There was something about boys' torsos, certain boys, that made Rosie look.

So, it was just the five of them there at first. The spring on the change room door creaked, Noah stepped inside and the

---

4   Constance explained a thing called the "male gaze" to me. Interesting stuff. This is my version of that, I guess.

door slammed behind him, and he slid the image of the red light into place. Occupied.

"No rude comments about the girls or I'll brain you," said Constance, settling onto her blanket, not even glancing at Walker when she said it.

"How about I put on your sunscreen, Connie?"

"I'd rather ask Heinrich Himmler."

"Nazi figure," said Bruce. "Second World War; Reichsführer of the Schutzstaffel, the SS, and the Geheime Staatspolizei, known as the Gestapo; architect of the final solution, destruction of the Jewish people; perhaps more ruthless than his leader, DER Führer, Adolf Hitler, father's original name Schicklgruber, erstwhile crappy painter, racist, good speaker. Himmler began as a chicken farmer and —"

"I think we get the picture, Brew. She'd prefer that I didn't apply the sunscreen."

"I'll do it," said Rosie.

Walker looked the other way, across the beach. He was staring again, but it was more intense than when he had glanced at Rosie. Miranda was coming and he had spotted her a mile away. Constance looked up too. Rosie turned. Miranda was like that. People always noticed her arrival. All the girls knew she deserved it too. She was gliding toward them in her quiet way, wearing a yellow sarong wrap over her suit, a book in hand, a thick one, of course.[5] All four watched her approach.

None of them saw Lisa Ann Bordeaux.

The spring on the change room door magically made no

---

5 Pretty sure it was *The Goldfinch* by Donna Tartt. She loved that book.

sound and neither did it slam as she let it close. In a breath, Lisa Ann was in there with Miranda Owens' boyfriend. That status was a big part of his attractiveness, that and the fact that Noah Greene had been revealed over these last few months to be exactly what Rosie Gonzalez had always known he was.

The change room, that place where you took off your clothes, was barely big enough for one person.

"Hi," was all Lisa Ann said to him at first, but there was a world of meaning in that word.

Miranda had begun to run when she saw her friends, somehow negotiating the sand as if it were a vulcanized track. She could fly. She seemed to get to them in no time. Three hugs and a nod at Walker, the thud of her book down onto her blanket, and she wanted to know about Noah.

"Where is he?" she asked with a smile, fixing her short, strawberry blond hair. Rosie was always amazed at how sensible, humble, and attractive she was, all at once. It seemed impossible. Miranda wasn't perfect. Her nose was a little too long, her figure probably too boyish, maybe a bit taller than many girls wanted to be, but there was something about her that drew you to her and shut up all the boys the instant she was nearby. It was some sort of charisma. It was in her sparkling, pale blue eyes, and in the way she moved, and it came from somewhere inside her. Miranda popped her sunglasses up, undid her sarong in one motion, letting it fall, and put her hands on her waist.

"Changing," said Constance, sounding bored and nodding toward the little blue building.

"Oh," said Miranda. "I'll surprise him."

She heard their voices as she approached, male and female inside the tight-quartered change room. His voice had become special to her; Lisa Ann's was distinctive too, like an alarm to other girls.

Miranda froze. She listened. Then she turned away, her face grim and down, her feet churning through the sand again, back toward her friends. As she moved, the door of the change room sprang open, loudly this time. Lisa Ann came tumbling out first, Noah behind her, his shirt and bathing suit still in hand, shoving her, though wrapped up in her too. Her hand still gripped his arm. She was dressed in a flowery little bikini.

"Get away from me!" he said to her.

Constance, Walker, Rosie, and Bruce stared. The first with a frown, the second with a riveted boy-stare at the flower pattern, and the other two in confusion.

"Come on, Noah," said Lisa Ann.

"Get away from me!" he shouted again.

Miranda turned on him. "EXACTLY what I was going to say!" she cried and marched away again, seizing her blanket and her sarong and beginning to move faster.

"Mir!" said Rosie. "Your book!" She picked it up and held it out to her friend.

Miranda stopped, hesitated, took a few strides back, ripped the book from Rosie's hand and started to run.

"Miranda!" shouted Noah. "Nothing happened! I promise you! I was trying to get away!"

Constance glanced at Lisa Ann, then back at Noah. "Poor boy," she said. "Under attack and helpless." She glared at him. "CREEP!"

"Nothing happened!" shouted Noah again after his vanishing girlfriend. People were staring now.

"Nothing happened?" said Walker. He gave Lisa Ann Bordeaux and her bikini another look. "Really?"

"SHUT UP, WALK!" Noah turned back toward Miranda; an expression of terror appeared to grow on his face.

"A boy and a girl in a change room together," said Bruce. "One in a small bathing costume, the other partially clothed."

"Are you all right, Noah?" asked Rosie. Her voice was barely audible.

"Are you serious, Rosie? Is HE all right?"

"Nothing did happen," said Lisa Ann with her hands on her hips, "unfortunately. Just a bit of fun, no big deal." She shrugged and began to walk away. "I think it's what he said," she said over her shoulder.

"What did you say?" asked Constance, her eyes now blazing at Noah.

NOAH CAUGHT UP TO Miranda on the boardwalk. He reached out and grabbed her arm. She instantly whirled on him and tore herself from his grip.

"Do not touch me!"

"Nothing happened! I know it looks bad that we were both in there but she —"

"You don't get it, do you? Guys don't get it, and I thought you were different!"

"What?"

"What you said! Do I have to spell it out? Though it's more than that too!"

"What did I say?"

She glared at him.

"I don't want to ever see you again, to hear your name, to even look at a book you've read; and you will certainly never, EVER touch me again! Do you understand me, Noah, you jerk?"

His face fell.

"Mir?"

"Leave me alone for the rest of my life!"

She stalked away. He stood there desolate for a moment, his world collapsing. When Miranda said something, she meant it. He felt tears coming. Then he remembered something she had said once about girls walking away in anger from boys in movies and the guys running after them, doing whatever it took to get them back. "I know it sounds stupid, but I love the idea of a guy running after me in that way."

He ran after her, his heart pounding. He couldn't believe how desperate he felt. It was as if his life, his very existence, depended on her taking him back. By the time he caught her again, she was off the boardwalk and out on the street near an ice cream stand. There were lots of people around. Everyone seemed happy. It was as if they were aliens. It was as if he were in a movie, a horror story. This time, when he reached out for her, she actually shoved him away, pushed him hard with both her hands on his chest, thrusting him back with Miranda Owens' undeniable power.

She wasn't even crying now. Her face was red and there was hatred in her eyes.

"I ...," he sputtered, trying to look optimistic, trying to

bring her irresistible smile to her face. "I ... I'm running after you ... calling you back."

"Fuck you, Noah Greene."[6] She didn't move when she said it, didn't flinch. She stood there and stared right at him.

He felt panic invade him. He dropped to his knees.

"I beg you," he said. "I love you."

"Oh, please, that is not possible. No one says what you said about a girl and loves her. You are a fraud. That's what you are to me: a fraud! You lied to me in the past and I ignored it, but now THIS! You had to be different, Noah, different from other guys. You HAD to be. But it turns out you aren't."

This time, she started to sprint. There wasn't a girl, and only a few boys, in the school who could catch Miranda Owens. Noah got up and ran after her for a while, crying now as he moved, his sense of well-being wrapped up in what would happen next. She ran along the sidewalk and cut dangerously across the main street, almost into the path of cars. On the other side, ripping past pedestrians and familiar stores where they had shopped together, she glanced back a few times to see him chasing her. He kept trying to keep up, though his body would barely obey him. By the time she reached the neighborhood two blocks from the far side of town, a block from her own, he stopped. He leaned on his knees, gasping, sobbing, wounded, embarrassed, and desperate. He thought she looked back for an instant right at the end, one last time, before she disappeared, but he wasn't sure.

Miranda Owens, THE Miranda Owens, the most amazing

---

6 That is a direct quote.

person he would ever meet, the most amazing love he had ever known and would ever know, had run out of his life. It was because of what he said.[7]

---

7 Obviously can't reveal this quite yet — I'd be a dunce if I let it out here. It's coming, though.

2
Where to Start

IT WAS BECAUSE OF who he was too. Noah Greene knew that.

He hadn't known who he was a few years ago. If the truth be told, he hadn't known who he was over the last eleven months either. That time had seemed like a dream, a fast, unbelievably happy dream. Before then, he had been living in reality, unmoored, but at least with some hope, however small, for the future. Now his dream was shattered and things were much worse. It was as if he were in hell. It had been a harsh world before her; it was going to be so much worse having lost her.

THE MOMENT HE FIRST saw her was like the first day of his life, and he had thought about it every day since then. Actually, it wasn't just seeing her. That was how it was different with Miranda. There was so much more than her physical presence that was overwhelming.

English class, first day of school, September 7.

"Hey," he said to the kid next to him, who was redheaded, dressed perfectly in a casual, black NBA logo tee, with rust-colored pants, tight at the ankles.

"Walker Jones," said the kid, looking up from his phone. He reached out and gave Noah one of those handshakes that come at you from an angle, gripping thumbs, palms slapping together — one that asks you to believe that its instigator is not a boring white guy. "Who are you?"

"Noah Greene. I'm new."

"No kidding. You're not in the cool section."

"Good."

Walker appeared to be unsure about how to react to that. He offered a weak smile.

"People call me Walk."

"Your crew?"

"They are legion."

That didn't seem to be true. Noah had sat in this particular spot in his homeroom because it was toward the back but not at the very back and because he was a little late and there was a seat available, beside Walker Jones. Students were still settling in, some still texting on their cells; the room was loud, the teacher still at the door talking to another one.

"I'll give you the lay of the land," said Walk. "Let's go around the clock." He dropped his voice and motioned to his left. "A few jocks at one o'clock; quarterback, first-line center, shooting guard, Lisa Ann in the middle of them. A couple of brains at three, some nerds at six, Miranda and her friends at nine, then us. We're at midnight, pumpkins."

Noah had stopped listening when he mentioned her name.

"Miranda who?"

"Oh," said Walker, smirking. "Forget about her."

"Why's that?"

"Because she's Miranda Owens. She's out of your league. She's perfect, but perfect in a not uncool way. That's nearly impossible, you know. She's smarter than the brains, at least in English, and cooler than the cool girls. She doesn't give a shit about what anybody thinks of her. She has her friends, weird friends if you ask me, and that's it."

"She's beautiful."

"I guess so. I think the better word is hot. You're right if that's what you mean. She sure doesn't flaunt it, though she could. She doesn't need to."

"Is she unfriendly?"

"No, no. Not at all. Very nice, but she mostly keeps to her friends, doesn't date anyone. A lot of the guys say gross stuff about her, but not a single one has the guts to say it anywhere near her or ask her out. I don't think she's ever had a boyfriend. No one is qualified. She's weird too, in other ways. She's got a cellphone, but no data — she only uses it like a phone!"

Noah tried not to stare at her. She was wearing loose-fitting clothing, unusual in a room where so many of the girls looked like they had nearly ironed-on their tops and pants. She didn't

wear a speck of makeup, either.[8] Her hair was short, as if cut
for practical reasons, not to impress anyone. Unusual too,
among rows of long-flowing, product-adjusted stylings. Her
nose was a little long, she seemed tall, almost gangly when she
was seated; her blue eyes, somehow, appeared to sparkle. On
top of everything, she was paying attention.

By the end of the day, Noah knew exactly how many classes
he shared with Miranda Owens: four out of six. History, Art,
Civics, and English. The last one was the most interesting, or at
least it became the most interesting to Noah because it was the
most interesting to Miranda.

The English class was called Twentieth Century English Literature and it started out with the usual suspects like Virginia
Woolf, Ernest Hemingway, and William Faulkner, and moved
all the way up to Toni Morrison and writers who are still alive,
like Margaret Atwood and John Irving. The teacher seemed
like a cool guy, wearing black-and-white Keds and a black
T-shirt with a picture of Edgar Allan Poe and a raven on it.[9]
He was actually asking everyone how they felt about the course
and if they could think of any novels that might be added, and
most of the students were saying things like "I don't know"
or "I guess it's good" or Noah's gem, which was "It sounds
interesting." A couple of people giggled at Noah's assessment,
not knowing that he was being genuine. Noah had peeked at

---

8   I found out later that she actually does wear some. Rosie let it slip once
    that she puts a bit of makeup on her face to conceal things, imperfections
    I guess, and something on her lips too, see-through gloss that looks natural,
    looks awesome, actually.
9   Referencing Poe's "The Raven," pub 1845, killer poem by a killer strange
    dude.

a few of the novels the teacher had mentioned when he used to get stuck in a library in the city last year waiting to meet his father, who always came past the building as he slouched home from whatever he was doing on any given evening. The waits could be long, so Noah had even read some of these novels almost all the way through, picking up about where he'd left off each time he was in the library. Some of the writing had seemed amazing to him. He had a bit of a thing for stories. He could understand where they were going and what made them tick. He always got good marks in English class. He could have gotten better ones, but he didn't want to stand out too much.

Miranda though, she was different, way different. When her turn came, she lit up. She launched into all sorts of ideas about things that could make the course better. She mentioned a bunch of female writers who might be added. "Right on," said this other girl, loud enough for all to hear, a girl with long, black curly hair and pale skin. Miranda said that maybe the teacher could add some "more challenging work" too, and mentioned a couple of "literary" novelists none of the others seemed to have heard of. She said it made sense because there was a grade twelve course offered next year called "Contemporary Literature" that was going to deal with important and complicated current writers like Zadie Smith, Hilary Mantel, Jonathan Franzen, and David Foster Wallace. She said that last guy's name slightly louder, as if he were an especially intriguing one to consider. No one appeared to have heard of him either.

The funny thing about her short speech was that it wasn't like a speech at all and no one made a peep while she talked.

Normally, at least in any of the other schools Noah had been in — and he had been in a boatload — half the class would have muttered snide comments under their breaths or snickered or rolled their eyes at anyone who said anything remotely like what Miranda Owens was saying. It wasn't that way at all with her. She spoke in an intense and passionate manner and yet did not seem to be showing off at all. She believed what she was saying. She didn't seem like a nerd or a brown-noser either. She was this sincere, interesting person, telling you how she really felt. At least, that was how Noah saw it.

He wanted to talk to her but couldn't work up the courage. He felt so far below her. It stayed that way for about a month.

THE DAY THEY FIRST broke the ice was auspicious in many ways. Noah had woken up in a good mood. That was a rare thing, especially on Thursdays, which that day was, and the other two days of the week when he was up late working at the grocery store. (Sometimes he felt like he could still smell the meat on his skin, which was impossible, since everyone in the freezer room wore aprons and gloves.) The apartment was always quiet in the morning. His father slept in every day and Mary Jane had been gone for several years, had left in between one of their moves in the city, so Noah rose alone and made his breakfast alone and made his way out the door alone every single time.

His eyes opened that day staring at his mother. She glowed back at him in black and white. He moved the photograph every night, hoping for this to happen, but it seldom did.

"Good sign," he said and immediately got up. That was a

rare thing too. Usually, he lay in bed for a while, sometimes a long while, thinking and thinking, his mind going in circles. He knew that wasn't a good thing. He had read somewhere online that moiling over things at night was a perfect way to sink yourself into depression or bring on anxiety. Sometimes, though, you can't stop yourself from doing the things that are bad for you. At least, that was what he used to think in those days, in the days "Before Miranda" and "During Miranda" and even during a good stretch of "After Miranda" too.

He looked around his bare room and felt his mood flatten. Same world as before. He didn't feel like showering. What was the point, really? He had showered yesterday. He pulled some jeans and a sweater over his slim frame — losing himself inside his clothes — slouched out into the little kitchen, and checked out the breadbox. It creaked as he opened it, so he stopped and peeked inside. Three slices of white bread, spots of mold like snot on the crust of every one. He would have to eat the Nutella straight from the jar.

His phone buzzed.

Come 4 breakfast. Mom is putting on a spread! B here or B square. U live kinda close, don't u?

Walker Jones to the rescue. Still his only real friend. Noah popped his phone back into the pocket of his jeans. He didn't have any data either, not something he was about to broadcast, though he'd had to tell Walk, said it was a choice. Noah squeezed his feet into his old black Vans and pulled on the jacket he was going to have to wear all winter. It was warm enough; many people had worse, people he had seen on the streets in the city. He opened the door gently and eased it shut

behind him before stepping out into the hallway. There was
a little echo and then silence. It seemed like no one else was
up yet. He headed toward the elevator, padding along the
bare carpet. "How long am I going to be able to keep Walk
away from here?" He pressed the button; there was a little
"ding" and a good minute or two later the door slid noisily
open. Empty. He got inside and the door closed, and the
elevator groaned, shrugged, and headed downward. "Maybe
I'll tell him how much I like going to his house, no need to
come here."

Outside in the crisp air he could see his breath, just about
right for mid-to-late October. Noah started toward Walk's
place.

"What if he finds out I work at the grocery store, meat
packing, late at night? What if a girl does ... Miranda Owens?"

He knew where the Joneses lived, had been there once or
twice. They were a nice family. Walker was struggling, though.
He was a good kid, unremarkable, a little shy, and a little
desperate to be liked at times, starved for peer affection. Noah
was happy to oblige him. They needed each other.

"I could be so much more," said Noah out loud, but quiet
enough so no one could hear him, as he left the apartments
area, concrete-dominated and parking-lot ridden, and headed
toward the Joneses' downtown suburb, which was full of big
trees and nice lawns. "I know I could. I look okay, I get looks
from girls, I seem to have a brain in my head. What's the point
though?"

The Jones family always greeted him as if he were their
long-lost friend or a dearly missed relative. Walk's mom was

Asian, his father as white as milk, and they made a loving and sometimes comical couple, bonded as they were to their decent but erratic and insecure only child.

"Mr. Greene, sir!" Mrs. Jones would call to him at the door, a lot shorter than him but much louder. She always seemed to answer when he knocked. "Shoes off like a good boy, please. Appetite large, like a good boy too! Proceed to the kitchen and destroy what we have prepared for you. Young Walker is at it now."

Noah took the hug that she offered — a strange thing for him since hugging was something he had not experienced since childhood, did not remember, really, and barely knew how to do. Then he slipped off his shoes and slid down the polished hard-wood floor in their small but immaculate bungalow, heading toward the enticing smell of bacon and eggs and other delights. The Joneses' home was like a warm warren to him, full of little corridors that emerged into small rooms — kitchen, living room, dining room, and the hall toward the two bedrooms.

"Hey!" said Mr. Jones, a big strapping fellow, the librarian at their school. "Noah without his ark!"

"Funny only the first seven times," said Walk. "Hey Noh, sit down! Engorge yourself!"

"We shall make use of the vomitorium should we need it," said Mr. Jones out of the side of his mouth, "and then eat more."

"Mrs. Jones heard that," said Mrs. Jones appearing out of a warren-hall into the bright back kitchen.

"It was a real thing, sweetheart," said her husband, "in Roman times."

"So was death by gladiatorial combat, dear. Let us enjoy our meal with Noah without employing such rude allusions."

"Such a lovely talker," said Mr. Jones as he gave his wife a kiss. "Science teachers are very sexy."

"Please," said Walk bringing his fingers up to his lips as if he were in danger of throwing up.

His mother then sat on his father's lap and gave him a long kiss.

"Take that," said Mrs. Jones. "Oh!" she cried, noticing that Noah was sitting in front of an empty place setting. "Get him some food!" She leapt off her husband who leapt up too, apron still on, and retrieved a plate full of eggs, bacon, toast, and tomatoes from a counter and deposited it in front of Noah.

"Thank you, Mr. and Mrs. Jones."

"You are quite welcome my dear. You are the nicest young man Walker has ever had over here. Eat up."

Probably never had anyone but me, thought Noah.

Walk's parents kept saying those sorts of incredibly nice things to him, pushing him to eat, giving him hugs, complimenting him, as if they could sense something: that he needed all that. Noah took it in. Walk was different. He appeared oblivious.

"NOT LOOKING FORWARD TO English class," Walker said as they left the house with both of their stomachs stretched from what they had loaded into themselves.[10]

"Why?" Noah could not imagine loathing English class.

---

10 I blame Mr. Jones for the five eggs I hoovered that day. I remember every one of them.

From where he sat, second row from the back, he had a perfect view of Miranda Owens in profile.[11]

"I cannot believe you even said that. I can sum up my dread in one word: Shakespeare. The most terrifying name in the English language."

"Oh, yeah."

"Oh, yeah? Is that all you can say? Billy Shakespeare, dude, the most boring man who ever set foot on earth! In fact, I think he's Satan's child, hatched by the Dark Lord so teachers can terrorize kids in high school with the crap he wrote. That's what we're doing today. Remember? That friggin' sleep-inducing play about the king and his daughters? Why does Mitchell even have him on the course? It's supposed to be Twentieth Century Literature and here he springs Billy-boy on us. I don't believe what he said about Shakespeare being 'modern' in a way and being the father of everything in literature now, and that he is going to show us how that's true. He just wanted an excuse to torture us. How can anyone consider a single word of that vomit to be modern? It's like it's Martian or something. I've been considering faking an illness on his 'Shakespeare Day' ever since he brought up his evil idea, but Mom and Dad figured out my acting long ago. I don't know if you had to go through any of Billy Shake's yawners last year, but we did. The thing was, in grade ten it was only an introduction to his drivel, so we read a couple of poems and studied a scene from this snore called *Hamet*."

"*Hamlet*."

---

11 Sorry. It's the truth, though.

"Did you study it too?"

"No."

"Then how do you know that?"

"I just do."

"You read it, didn't you?"

"Yeah, some of it."

"Most of it?"

"Yeah."

"Man, I cannot figure you out. You probably read this whole *King Lear*[12] thing too."

"Skimmed some, but got through a lot of it."

"And didn't Mitchell say something about finishing the course with *another* Shakespeare play?"

"*The Tempest.*"

"Great. Maybe I'll lick a toilet seat the week before and get a real illness."

"Relax."

"Relax? I couldn't even get past the first page. I couldn't understand a word!"

"You don't have to. Just let it flow. It's beautiful stuff, really. Just let it flow and stop worrying about understanding all of it. It's about the importance of the truth. It's a cool story."

Walk stopped in his tracks and Noah didn't realize it for a few seconds. When he turned back, Walk was staring at him.

"Cool? What, are you, like, an alien?"

It wasn't something Noah would have said to anyone else,

---

12 *The Tragedy of King Lear*, first performed in 1606 in London, England. Man, that's, like, way over 400 years ago and here we were talking about it in the streets! Pretty impressive.

but it was okay to tell Walk things like this.

"Yeah, it's cool."

"All right, explain it to me. Now!"

"That's impossible."

"Not the whole friggin' meaning of the thing, just what happens, the CliffsNotes of the story."

"No."

"What do you mean, 'no'? Are you my friend or not?"

"I am your friend, Walk, that's why I am not going to explain it to you. Read it yourself. You can do it."

"I cannot do it!" He actually screamed that out. They had reached the main street, still lined by residential homes, big old ones owned by rich people, their school about ten minutes away. They had also begun to encounter a few pedestrians. In fact, from where Noah was standing, looking back at Walk again, he could see three girls, fairly popular ones, wearing black leggings and light tops in the freezing cold. They had looked up from their phones and were staring at Walk from behind, frowning, acting as if his uncool shout was typical for a jerk like him. Walk turned around and saw them. He froze. They passed by. Noah felt he needed to say something nice to him.

"There's a battle in it. You'll like that," he said quietly.

The girls were out of earshot now. Noah and Walker started moving again.

"A battle? Okay, who wins and how many people die? Do we get to see lots of blood?"

"There's a fool in it too."

"A fool? You mean, like a clown. So, it's funny in places?"

"Um ... not sure I would say that."

"Tell me more."

"No. You need to read it. You can do it. Any kid can do it. You just have to try. Making an effort is important in life."

"Are you suddenly, like, some sort of self-help guru or something?"

"No, I just think that people can do and be more than they think they can. The play talks about that too."

"Man, to you it talks about everything."

"Yeah, it sort of does. So, uh, so did *Hamlet*. And *The Tempest* is even better."

For a second, Noah thought Walk was going to slug him.

MIRANDA OWENS LOOKED PARTICULARLY happy that day. Noah could remember that clearly. It seemed to him that she was sort of glowing, if that is at all possible.

"I know that a number of you will not have read *King Lear*," said Mr. Mitchell, "even though I asked you to start into it a week ago and to be finished by today."

Mitchell was like that all the time. He was down-to-earth, realistic about teenagers, and students liked him for it. "That's okay ... sort of. It is at least, shall I say, understandable. Shakespeare can be rather daunting. Really though, that's just a surface impression. In his day, his plays were popular and the average person came to see them. They actually have all sorts of jokes in them, wordplay for average playgoers, some of them dirty jokes, to be honest."

There were a couple of snickers in the class.

"So, remember that if you tried to read it and got flustered and just could not go on. Try it again and understand what you can; read it and try to get into the story. Remember what we said at the beginning of the year: Story. That is what matters in everything we talk about in this class, no matter how complicated the text. This is a great story. That is why it has lasted. All human beings like stories; every one of us. It is undeniable. Our own lives are stories. We all are protagonists in our own drama. Shakespeare understood that … every which way. It is the basis of everything he wrote and he was the greatest writer who ever lived."

Kids were shuffling in their seats, some looking up at the ceiling, others gawking at each other. Noah glanced over at Miranda. Her attention was locked onto Mr. Mitchell. Noah had been doing well in this class. He always did well in English. He had been getting nineties on everything he'd written for Mitchell so far. No one knew that, of course, not even Walk. Noah hadn't spoken much in class. But at that moment, looking over at the incandescent Miranda Owens, seeing her fascinated by the words coming out of Mitchell's mouth, thinking about what he'd said to Walker Jones about the importance of trying to improve yourself, he made a decision.

"Can anyone tell me anything about *King Lear*?" asked Mitchell. "It doesn't matter what you say or how much understanding of the text you have. Tell me anything. It will be good to hear whatever you say."

There was silence in the class. Miranda looked around. It was obvious that she wanted someone to speak up, that she didn't want to be the one who held forth, again. She didn't look as anxious as she often did and that was partly because of the nature of Mitchell's question. He was giving the kids who didn't understand the story, didn't have a clue really, a chance to speak. It was like he was giving the groundlings, the ordinary people who stood on the ground at the Globe Theatre in London way back in the day and laughed at Shakespeare's crude jokes, a chance to talk.

Walk's hand went up.

"Yes, Walker?" asked Mitchell, looking pleased.

"I like the battles, the action."

"Very good. So do I. Anything else?"

Walk glanced at Noah. "The clown is good too."

"The clown? Do you mean the fool?"

"Yeah, the fool, that's right. He's funny."

Mitchell paused. "Funny? Uh ... I suppose, in a way, but he is much more than that — a whole lot more. Do you agree?"

"Uh ... yeah. He's cool."

There were a few snickers. Mitchell sought the authors of that reaction and frowned at them. "Anyone else?"

Constance put up her hand. "I like the fact that there are some women in the story, in key roles. That's a rare thing in all these dead white guy stories we have to read from the days of the patriarchy ... which is ongoing." There were a couple of male groans in the class. "Even with the women having some good roles here, though, I don't think they are respected enough. Parts of the play are a sort of boys' club thing. There's the king and then there are the daughters, but it is really the king we are focused on."

"Okay," said Mr. Mitchell. "Interesting comment. I can tell you have put some thought into it. Now, can anyone tell me what happens in the story?"

There was silence for a few seconds. Then Bruce thrust up his hand. He rarely answered anything.

"Yes, Bruce. You don't need to tell us everything; the first scene will be fine."

Bruce was shaking and his voice was quavering too.

"W-We open in a k-kingdom long ago where a king, the aforementioned Mr. L-Lear, is thinking about being old and maybe passing on his crown. He asks his three d-daughters how much they l-love him and the first two b-bullshit him ..."

There was a roar of laughter.

"Quiet!" shouted Mitchell, who had never raised his voice in class before. When there was silence, he smiled. "That's fine, Bruce, you are absolutely correct, please go on."

But Bruce was shaking too much. Miranda stood up. She never did that. No one did. You sat to answer a question. She wanted the entire class's attention on her, though, not on her poor shaking friend. This, in a snapshot, was Miranda Owens, and Noah sat transfixed.

"Bruce is right," she said, "and insightful. The two daughters do answer their father with bullshit." There was dead silence in the class when that word came out of her mouth and she made sure she pronounced it clearly. Mr. Mitchell smiled again. "But Cordelia, the third and youngest daughter, doesn't; she tells him the truth. He can't handle it. The story goes on from there, an amazing tale of Lear casting out his daughter, cozying up to the ones who just want something from him, and then descending into drinking and rabblerousing. He is accompanied by his Fool, who keeps telling him what is really going on, and finally, he is involved in battle, yes, blind and distraught, saved at the end by realizations about life, and about how much his truthful daughter really loves him. It tells us about maturing, the wisdom of old age, or at least the wisdom we all should acquire then, by our experiences." She sat down.

In the ensuing silence, a quiet voice said, "Sir?"

The new kid who had barely uttered a word over the first month or so of classes had his hand up. The kid who Mr. Mitchell knew had a way with stories but had never offered anything remotely like his essays in front of the class.

"Yes, Noah?"

"I noticed a few things in the text."[13]

"Go on."

Out of the corner of his eye, he could see Miranda turning in her seat to watch him.

"Though I enjoyed the story itself, it is so much more than that. It is about an old man, yes, and wisdom, but more importantly it's about vision. It's about truly seeing others, cutting through the surface, the role-playing we all do, all of that, understanding others. I noticed, as I re-read it, how often Shakespeare uses the word 'I' or 'eye' or in some way references selfishness, vision, or sight. I also noticed that as the play progresses, the old king's eyesight worsens, and in the end he is blind. It is only when he can't see that he truly sees. It is only then that he encounters his daughter Cordelia ... and truly sees her. I'm not sure this is a lesson to learn or anything like that — I don't think Shakespeare is into that. It's simply a truth. Great art tells the truth."

---

13 Sweating bullets and nearly crapping my pants at this point.

Noah finished to another silence. Miranda Owens was staring at him, absolutely staring, and he knew it.

"I ... I," said Mr. Mitchell, "I have never, in all my years teaching this text, noticed that. That is ... that is amazing. Thank you, Noah. I mean that ... thank you."

When all the other students had turned back to the front, Miranda was still looking at Noah. It took her a good ten seconds to turn around again at her desk.

AS THEY LEFT THE class that day, she approached him.

"Whoa," said Walk into Noah's ear. "She's coming this way."

"Noah?" she said. She came right up close, her eyes looked right into his. He noticed that he was only an inch or two taller. "That was awesome." And she put her hand on his arm for a second and then was gone.

"Holy Moses," said Walk. "Holy flippin' Moses!"

3
A Meeting of Mind and Body

NOAH WAS SURPRISED WHEN he heard that Miranda was on the basketball team, since that isn't where you usually expect to find "A" students.[14] She also didn't hang out with the jocks and never wore any hoops gear. Sweatpants and logos were not her thing. She didn't act like a jock, talk like one, or move like one. Well, maybe she moved like one. She had a different way of walking, at least it seemed to Noah that she did. She seemed to move effortlessly, gracefully. She never appeared to be showing off anything about her appearance — her body, either. She was always wearing those loose-fitting clothes. She favored sweaters and relaxed-fit jeans, and rarely even bared her arms. She dressed for comfort.

So, it was a revelation to see her play basketball.

---

14 Stereotyping, I know, sorry, there are definitely some smart jocks, this works for the story though.

In a way, he wasn't proud of going to the game. He knew that part of him wanted to see her in the team's shorts and top.[15] A small part of him, but it was there. Walk definitely did. He let that out the instant Noah brought up the idea of going to a game.

School got out an hour early on game days and all the students were supposed to attend, but many didn't, especially when the girls were playing.[16]

Noah had been thrilled by what Miranda said to him and by her touch, but also by the way she gazed at him. She seemed to be almost trying to look into him — a questioning, penetrating peer.

He made up his mind at that moment that he was going to watch her play.

"Up for some Black Ops at my place?" asked Walk as they closed up their lockers that day.

"I think I'm going to the game."

"What?"

"The girls' game."

That was probably when Walk started imagining Miranda — and some of the other girls — in their shorts and tops.

"Right on," he smiled.

Unfortunately, the first person they encountered at the gym was Constance Mark.

"Well, look at what we have here," she sneered, loudly, sitting next to Bruce and a girl named Rosie Gonzalez, making up about a quarter of the entire crowd on that side of the

---

15 Sorry. Sounds bad, I know, but in novels, you have to be truthful.
16 Which sucks.

bleachers. Constance was constantly on the guys in her class to come to these games. "What's the attraction?" she asked, loudly again, then glanced out toward Miranda and the other girls who were warming up.

"Go away," said Walk, under his breath.

"I heard that, Jones. The truth is a bit too much for you, isn't it? Typical."

But Miranda wasn't sneering. It was obvious to Noah that she was trying to focus on what she was doing, like she always did, but he also noticed that she noticed him. As she rebounded a ball under the basket and made her way out to the foul line for a jump shot, she caught sight of him sitting down with Walker. She missed the shot. He had the feeling that didn't happen often.

Much to his shame, he did not pay a lot of attention to her form — at least not to her shooting form. There she was ... no longer in loose clothing. To Noah, and, he had to guess, to every other heterosexual male in the universe, she was spellbinding. She wasn't the tallest player on the team, she was just above average, and yet there was nothing average about her. She was ... well, he couldn't describe it. Everything about her seemed the way it ought to be. She was like the golden mean or the golden ratio or divine geometry or whatever that thing was in mathematics, architecture, and nature, where everything looked beautiful and balanced.[17] She wasn't perfect and yet she was. Once the ball was tipped to start the game, she was all business, or mostly so.

---

17 I hope this also doesn't sound too bad, "male gaze," or objectifying. It's the way I feel, though. Can't help it.

It seemed to Noah that she was aware that he was there even as she played. She did well, as she apparently always did, but somewhere in her alert eyes, in her perspiring face, in the very language of her movements, she knew he was watching her. It was so exhilarating that he did not have the words to describe it. He felt like they were doing this together, like he, sitting in the crowd, and she, running on the court in another crowd, were communicating with each other. Some sort of chemical invasion was happening to him too. He felt like he was weightless and simultaneously heavy. He felt so happy that he almost couldn't stay upright. He had the sense that out there in the game, she felt the same way.

When the buzzer sounded at the end, he wanted to walk out onto the court and talk with her as she celebrated with her teammates. He wanted to take her into his arms. It turned out that wasn't needed because she turned in the midst of the celebration and smiled at him. He smiled back.

"Man, what is going on?" asked Walk as they left the gym. "Miranda Owens was smiling at you! It's like ... like ... she's in love with you or something."

That sounded weird coming out of Walker Jones's mouth. It was as if the word "love" and definitely the words "in love" were from some sort of foreign language that he had no idea existed, let alone how to pronounce.

Noah was flustered. "Let's go," he said before bounding down off the bleachers, turning toward the exit, and then picking up the pace in the hallway, making Walk nearly run to keep up. They pushed through the outside doors and felt the sun shining down on them. It had been so different on the way to school in the morning. It was surreal; the cold fall day had transformed into a strangely warm late afternoon. "Let's go to your place. I want to shoot hoops."

It had become their thing during their first month or so of friendship. Walk had a net in his driveway and he had lowered it a bit, just below standard height, so he might have an outside chance at dunking. He never did, of course, not even at that height, though Noah had come close. All through September and into October they had banged around, stripping down to shorts and skins, Noah destroying Walk each and every time, no matter what game they played or challenge they tried.

"You're good," Walk had said to him more than once. "You should have tried out for the team."

It wasn't Noah's thing, though.

Noah felt awfully strange that day as they made their way to Walk's house. Now, he couldn't tell if he was happy or angry or what. He did know he was frustrated. He couldn't get Miranda out of his mind. Not the look she gave him, the sound of her voice, or the way she moved with the ball in her hands on the court. He felt like he wanted to sprint to the end of the earth ... or jump off a cliff.

They walked home in silence.

"You're a talkative bastard," Walk finally said. "Why are you so —"

"No reason."

"Right."

"If I say I have no reason for being quiet, then I mean it!"

He drew to a halt when he said that and glared at Walker

Jones. Those words were the first angry ones that had passed between them. Walk looked a little scared.

"Okay," he said quietly.

Miranda Owens was untouchable, unknowable, and unreachable. She was beyond Noah Greene, and he wanted to hit something.

HE TOOK IT TO Walk like he never had before on their little driveway court. He pushed him around, he dribbled past him as if he were standing still, and he even ran him over a couple of times. Every shot he tried to make, he made. He schooled him.

"Give me a chance, LeBron," said Walk at one point.

Noah was perspiring like a fiend. He took off his shirt. Scrawny Walker Jones did the same.

Then Noah did it.

He dunked.

Noah saw that Walk was leaning to his left, knowing that Noah usually went right, so Noah faked left, drew Walk that way, then took two steps and rose up above him like Michael Jordan in old clips. He slammed the ball down through the net with two hands, nearly tearing the basket off the backboard.[18] They both stood and stared at what he had done, the hoop still vibrating. Then, they started to laugh, but it didn't last long.

They realized that someone — four people, in fact, were standing out on the sidewalk at the end of the driveway staring at them. Noah, however, only saw one. Miranda.

---

18 Perhaps I exaggerate.

She was gazing at him as he stood shirtless and sweating, back on land after accomplishing his moonshot. Walker grabbed his shirt and threw it back on. Beside Miranda stood Constance Mark, Bruce King, and Rosie Gonzalez.

Then something equally ridiculous happened. Miranda started coming toward them. Well, toward Noah. She was smiling again, but not quite the same smile she had given him back in the gymnasium; this one was a little more self-conscious, shy, but it had the same effect on him. He had not known that Miranda could ever look shy around anyone. *Wow*, thought Noah, *am I doing that to her?* He could feel himself rising up into the air, watching all of this happen in slow motion. His heart began to pound.

"Hi," she said.

"Hi," he somehow got out. She looked at him as if Walk wasn't there, as if her friends had faded into the distance.

"Nice dunk," she said. "I didn't know you could ..."

"Play ball?"

"Yeah."

"I can't."

She laughed. "That's not true."

"Walk lowered the basket."

"Still, that was impressive."

"Come on, Mir!" shouted Constance from the sidewalk. "Let's go."

"Can I play with you?" asked Miranda.

Noah tried to answer, but nothing came out.

"Uh," said Walker, "it's just me and —"

"Sure," said Noah.

By this time, Constance and the other two had come up the driveway.

"An interesting challenge in the game of basketball. A boy against a girl," said Bruce.

Miranda grinned at him and then back at Noah. "Do you want to do that? Me against you?"

"Sure."

She took off her hoodie and tossed it on the ground. "My ball first."

He let her go by him and score. As she corralled the ball and passed him on her way back to the foul line, she came up close. "Don't do that," she said heatedly. She was deadly serious, not pleased with him. It was like a command. There was something anxious in her voice too, as if she were worried that he was not measuring up or something.

He almost knocked her into the garage door the next time she tried to go by him, rising up as she passed the ball smoothly and low to the ground from her right hand to her left, and raising it to try a hook shot. He swatted the ball with everything he had, sending it crashing into a garbage can and incidentally knocking her backward.

"Isn't that a penalty or something?" asked Constance. "That's not fair."

Miranda was smiling. She had smoothly regained her balance. "He got the ball first. All ball. No foul."

He dunked on her. When he landed, they were inches apart, his skin almost touching her T-shirt. They both paused for a second. She smelled good. How was that even possible after this sort of physical exertion?

Once, she touched his bare chest when it seemed she didn't need to. "Sorry," she said, but it was almost as if she didn't mean it. "That's all right," he responded, and they grinned at each other.

She was a handful, of course. He didn't beat her every time he tried, and she scored on him several times, but in the end, he triumphed, ten to six. He was amazed at how good she was when he tested her — she was strong and never gave an inch. She was graceful and talented. It made him realize that he was pretty good too.

"Can we go now?" asked Constance.

"We don't have to," said Rosie, who was staring at Noah, somehow doing so while barely looking at him.

"No," said Miranda. "I've got to go. I told Mom I'd be home by 6:30." She picked up her hoodie and draped it over an arm. Her face was wet with perspiration. "Thanks for the game," she said to Noah. "I'll beat you next time." It was obvious to Noah how competitive she was, that she had not liked the fact that she had lost; he could tell by the way she had played, the way she had strained to win, the slight anger in her face and in some of her aggressive moves. Yet there was also something in her expressions that was happy too — not to lose, but to have him engage her so honestly.

"Next time?" said Constance.

"Another occasion of playing the game of basketball to-gether, just the two of them likely during that occurrence," said Bruce.

"I get that," muttered Constance.

The four of them started making their way down the

driveway, but before they reached the end, Miranda turned and walked back toward Noah.

"Can I, uh, talk to you for a second?"

He shot the ball at the hoop, swish, and walked over to her. They talked for a moment in low voices. They smiled at each other as they parted, Miranda looking right at him, he glancing at her and then down at the ground.

Miranda and her friends were gone for nearly five minutes, and Noah had scored ten more points on his poor opponent before Walk finally asked him.

"What did she say?"

"Not much."

They played a little more.

"What do you mean 'not much'?"

Noah fired the ball at him, chest high. Walk barely got his hands up in time.

"She asked me out."

Walk dropped the ball. It dribbled on the pavement and rolled onto the backyard.

"She *what*? Miranda Owens?"

Noah picked up his shirt, put it on, grabbed his backpack, threw it over his shoulder, and walked off down the driveway, heading home.

"See you later," he said over his shoulder.

"Nice exit," said Walk to himself. "I'd give my left nut to do that someday, all of that." He retrieved the ball and went to his back door. As he entered, to the friendly cries of "hello" from both his mother and father, he thought about Noah Greene. What did he have that would make a girl like that, an unbelievable girl like that, want to ask him out? What did he have other than one lucky answer to a question in class or the way he looked shirtless? Maybe that was it, that last part. He doubted it, though. He wondered, too, why Noah never asked him over to his place.[19]

---

19 Being a novelist here, I made this up, felt like a moment like this worked well in the story. Besides, I know Walk well and I'm guessing he was thinking something like this. That "left nut" thing is an expression of his. Painful to contemplate.

4
First Dates

SHE CHOSE WHERE THEY went on their first date and paid for it too. That didn't surprise Noah and he wasn't complaining, not at all, especially since he didn't have enough money in his pocket to pay for a chocolate bar. Every cent he made at the grocery store went to rent. It was the day after they played basketball together, that Friday. Thank God she hadn't picked a Monday, Wednesday, or Saturday. He remembered that night well, always will. October 22. Twenty-two: two twice. Miranda and Noah, an exceptional two, a couple.

They went to a little café in a bookstore in town. It was cool, or at least they both thought so. The floors were wood and creaked when you walked on them, the shelves looked like they were from the Hogwarts library or Victorian England, with sliding ladders so you could reach the books at the top. There was also a movie theater upstairs. It showed mostly old

flicks. There was one scheduled for that day that she liked.
They ended up in the tight seating up there, holding hands.
He hadn't said a word about not wanting to see this particular film when she brought up the idea while they ate. It was
a romance — she'd made that clear; one called *Breakfast at
Tiffany's*.[20] She had taken his hand the second they sat down in
a row at the back. She'd bought the popcorn too.

"So," she said, as they clomped down the rickety stairs afterward with the dozen other people who had attended, all of
them adults, many of them gray-haired, "what did you think?"

"Very interesting," he said.

"Really?"

"Not your average love story."

"How would you know?"

"Good point."

She laughed and took his hand again.

He realized that he needed to explain. "I guess what I
meant was that when I watch a movie, I find myself following
the writing, if that makes sense, and it seems to me that this
one was interestingly written. It wasn't a straightforward arc.
There were some interesting lines too, like the one where the
woman talks about her independence and says — 'I'll never let
anyone put me in a cage.'"

Miranda squeezed his hand.

When they reached her house, a nice old one in an old part
of town, she didn't invite him in. She did, however, kiss him as

---

20 Starring Audrey Hepburn and George Peppard, novel by Truman Capote,
an awesome author. Movie was great, the book was even better, as is
always the case.

they stood on the big veranda with the love-seat swing right beside them. At first, it seemed as if she was actually going to shake his hand and then simply turn toward her door, but instead she pulled him toward her, moved in, and then immediately backed away.

"Sorry," she said.

He looked at her for a moment, shocked by what she had done, and said, "What do you mean 'sorry'?"

"I hadn't intended to do that. I'll see you tomorrow." She was through her door and inside in a flash.

Noah did not really walk home that night. It was as if he floated there, his feet not touching the ground, his mind a blissful blank. "Miranda," he kept repeating, over and over again. "Miranda."

WORD SPREAD FAST THAT they were dating. The other students, and even the teachers, were stunned. The girls were beyond freaked-out. Many of them, somehow, knew all about it before Miranda Owens even came back to school the day after her basketball game, dressed again in her uncool clothes but looking infuriatingly cool, and holding hands with Noah Greene. Noah Greene! It was unbelievable. It was frickin' ginormously impossible. Then again, by the end of the day, many of the girls were texting that this new guy, actually, when you looked a little harder, and thought about him a bit more, was awfully cute. A rumor even began to circulate that he had a killer bod underneath those loose clothes.[21]

---

21 Rosie told me all of this too, turning red, again.

They didn't kiss in the halls or get too touchy-feely. That did not seem to be their style. They just appeared to talk a lot. They laughed, they did that thing where you stare at each other quite a bit, but they didn't show off their attraction to each other, not at all. It was weird.[22]

Their second date truly got people talking. They went to the library. The students who saw them there said that it looked like a real, honest-to-goodness date. At the library. Not a single kid, however, knew what they did afterward. They went to the gym, just the two of them. They were not supposed to be there. No one was. The room was dark, the balls were all on a cart, but Miranda and Noah sneaked in, turned on the lights, piled their books and homework in the stands, and played one-on-one again.

This time he won ten to seven. It got a little nasty too. He was getting physical with her, shoving her around in order to try to shut her down. So, she elbowed him in the face. Not intentionally, or at least it didn't look that way. It backed him off a little and she won the next three points. When he scored the last basket, the one that ended the game, they looked like they were mad at each other, but she took him into her arms in a few seconds and squeezed him like she never had before, in a sweaty hug, and kissed him longer too.

"Thanks," she said.

Then they heard a voice, a big, male one, booming at them from the other end of the gym.

"Excuse me," he said.

---

22 To others.

"Oh no," said Noah under his breath, "we're in trouble."

It was Mr. Beatty, the senior boys' basketball coach, but he wasn't angry, not at all.

"Mr. Greene?" he asked.

"Yes, sir," said Noah, gulping, and quickly stepping back from his playing partner.

"Hey, Miranda," he said.

"Hey," she replied, unconsciously fixing her short hair.

"Get a load of this guy, eh," said Beatty.

"Sorry, sir, this was my idea, I —"

"Where you been hiding?"

"I wasn't hiding, I —"

"I mean, where have you been hiding all that talent? It would be a challenge for me these days to beat Miss Owens here one-on-one and I played second division college ball."

"Maybe in your prime you'd stand a chance," said Miranda.

Beatty smiled at her and turned back to Noah. "You know, Mr. Greene, we have a couple of ailing players right now. Why don't you come out to practice tomorrow after school?"

"Uh, no, I have things to —" he began, but could feel Miranda's gaze on him. "Uh, sure," he finally said.

"Excellent," said Beatty. "Now, if you two can be out of here in ten seconds, then one second after that I will have completely forgotten that you were ever in here without supervision."

THE THIRD DATE HAD a lot to it.

"How about another movie on Friday night at the book-store?" asked Miranda when they met at his locker the next day.

"Sure," he smiled.

"Would it be okay," she said slowly, her eyes looking down and then flashing up at him to meet his as she caressed the sleeve of his warm checked shirt, "if it were a mob date?"

"A what?"

"If a whole bunch of us went. You could invite your friends and I could invite mine."

"In that case, there would be thousands; football stadiums couldn't hold them."

She laughed a little, then laughed more, and put her head on his chest and hugged him. "Yes, veritable phalanxes of our followers and loved ones."

"Armies of our dearest associates."

"Yes, you with ... let me see," she scratched her chin. "Ah yes, Walker Jones and ..."

"Walker Jones."

"The most popular man in the school."

"And you with Rosie and Constance."

"... and Bruce."

That omission was a mistake and he quickly corrected it. He had hardly ever said a word to Bruce. "Of course."

She kissed him quickly and when she pulled back, she stared right into his eyes, their faces barely inches apart as she seemed to look into him again. Blue eyes like the sky on a perfect day, a few perfectly placed freckles, strawberry blond hair. He felt like he could still feel her face; still feel her skin on his from two inches away. He could smell her, too; she had that "Miranda" scent. For an instant, he was so happy that he felt he might faint. She seemed to sense that, all of it, and her eyes watered. There was some sort of promise in her reaction and it thrilled him beyond description.

"Tonight," she said. He turned and watched her glide away in her loose jeans. She looked back for an instant. "Parting is such sweet sorrow," she mouthed and grinned, and he got every word.

WHEN THEY MET AT the front door of the bookstore that night, he had Walk in tow, but she only had Rosie and Bruce.

"Here they come," said Noah as he and his buddy noticed the other three turning a corner a block away and advancing toward them. He had wanted to wear something a little tighter today, show off his body a bit, which he knew was at least of some interest to girls. He had noticed a few looks. Miranda seemed to notice too, though she never said anything. He was a good height for his age, lean but reasonably muscular, and he sometimes looked at himself in a mirror without his clothes on and imagined the effect it might have.[23] He imagined it at least would not be negative. He had chosen his baggier jeans though and a loose black sweater. Something told him that Miranda would appreciate that. He was surprised though at what she was wearing. Her red top was a fairly thin blouse and her belly button showed when she turned or lifted her shoulders. He had never seen her in anything like that. She was smiling at him from way down the street, focused on him. It did not seem real. He looked around, as if to confirm that he was not on a movie set.

Walk was wearing some sort of cologne.

---

23 Don't laugh!

"What the hell is that?" Noah had asked him when he dropped by the Joneses' house so they could walk to the movie.[24]

"What do you mean?"

"That smell."

"I don't smell anything."

"Yeah, because you're doused in it."

Walk seemed nervous. When Noah invited him and told him who was coming, he could actually see him swallow, the Adam's apple moving up and down in his throat. Walk had texted about five times confirming the time they would meet and was still tense as they waited at the bookstore, standing on one foot then the other, fidgeting with his shirt and smoothing it out. When he noticed the other three approaching, he said, "That's a relief."

"What do you mean?"

"No Constance Mark, thank God."

He seemed a little less nervous then. "What's the deal with this movie?"

"The deal?"

"What's it about? Who's in it?"

"Don't know and don't know."

"You mean you asked me to come to a movie with you and YOU know zero about it?"

"Miranda said it was good. She has good taste. It's an old one; she likes old ones. I think it's a sort of horror flick, or at least really intense. It'll be cool."

Walk glanced at the poster.

---

24 This despite the fact that my apartment was closer to the bookstore.

"*Rear Window*," he said aloud.

Though Noah leaned toward Miranda as the others arrived, she didn't kiss him. She took him by the hand and smiled. He wondered if he should say something about the blouse, but decided against it. The fact that she kept smiling at him seemed to indicate that was the right decision.

"Hi, Walker," said Rosie.

"Hi."

"Hello," she said to Noah, blushing a little.

"I'm glad you could come too, Rosie," he said and briefly put his hand on her shoulder. He could feel her shiver when he touched her.

"Good evening, Mr. Walker Jones and Mr. Noah Greene. It is a wonderful evening to view a film."

"Hi Bruce," said Noah, taking his hand as he offered it. Bruce shook hands with Walk too, who looked down while they did it.

"Where's Constance?" asked Noah.

"Uh, we had a little disagreement about the film."

"What do you mean?"

"Uh, this movie was directed by Alfred Hitchcock."

"He was awful to women," said Rosie quietly, "or at least that's what some people who worked for him said."[25]

"I've read that," said Noah. "He was almost abusive to them on set."

---

25 Hitchcock seemed to have a sort of fetish about his leading women in his movies. He wanted them all to be beautiful and blond. He put them into horrifying situations in scenes, and made that real for them, sometimes terrorizing them. At least one actor said he assaulted her.

"You might be able to ditch the *almost*."

"Anyway," said Miranda, "this movie was made way back in 1954, in Technicolor. I saw it about a year ago when Mom had it on and she let me watch too. I don't really like horror stories, or overly intense ones, most of them are stupid, but I like psychological terror. I think the greatest horrors are in your own mind."

"Won't bother me," said Walk. "Bring it on." He looked at the two girls as he said this, as if to gauge their reaction.

"I get why Constance didn't come," said Miranda. "Totally. Especially because Hitchcock had power over the women who were his victims. I try to separate the art from the artist when I'm reading and watching movies, though. Sometimes it's tough to do. There are some creepy artists out there. But a great book isn't not important because some less-than-stellar guy wrote it. I'm just here to see *Rear Window* and I can tell you, it's amazing."

Rosie was gazing up at her.

"Picasso was an asshole," said Noah.

Rosie laughed. Miranda smiled. Walk looked blank.

"Pablo Picasso, artist, master of cubism, genius," said Bruce. "Born 1881 Málaga, Spain, died 1973, Mougins, France. Creator of *Guernica*, *Les Demoiselles d'Avignon*, and *Weeping Woman*. They are just some of his many masterpieces."

Miranda put her had gently on his shoulder to stop him from going on.

She and Noah were virtually leaning into each other while she bought their tickets. "Don't you need a warmer coat tonight?" she said a moment later, as they entered the theater.

"This one is fine, an old favorite. It's much warmer than it seems."

THEY LINED UP THIS way in the second-last row: Walk, then Noah, Miranda, Rosie, and Bruce. Miranda gripped Noah's hand almost from the opening credits and never let go. There were moments during the action when he thought she was going to break his fingers. She had good reason.

Though it started quaintly, it slowly became terrifying. At first, it was simply about an ordinary guy named Jeff (played by James Stewart) who was confined to a wheelchair in his stiflingly hot city apartment while recovering from an injury. He sits around all day looking out his big back window and through the windows of other apartments, right into their interiors, across a courtyard. His girlfriend, Lisa (played by Grace Kelly), often visits him, but he isn't very nice to her and dwells on his own concerns. He starts noticing a big, scary-looking man in one of the apartments across the way who has violent arguments with his wife. Eventually, Jeff starts observing them close up, through binoculars. One night in a thunderstorm, he hears a scream from the couple's apartment. The next day the man's wife is gone and then Jeff sees him disposing a large body-sized trunk. A dog starts sniffing around in the courtyard soil beneath the man's apartment and in the night, someone breaks its neck. Jeff sends Lisa out to investigate when the suspected murderer is away. Then things get truly intense. Finding nothing, Lisa recklessly climbs the fire escape and enters the man's room ... and as she does, while Jeff watches, the man unexpectedly returns! He attacks Lisa, the violence soundless and distant, Jeff helplessly writhing in his chair, his eyes wide with terror, pleading aloud that she be spared, but his voice is unheard. He finally hits on a desperate plan, struggles to a phone, and calls the police. The officers arrive before she is murdered, and arrest her for breaking and entering, which at least removes her from immediate danger. As she leaves, she flashes her hand across the courtyard toward Jeff and his binoculars ... she is wearing the dead wife's wedding ring, which she had found buried in the dirt below! The murderer notices and Jeff sees that he does! The man's evil eyes glare back across the courtyard! Moments later, the killer is thudding up the stairs toward the wheelchair-bound Jeff in his apartment! It was during the next moments that Miranda nearly broke every one of Noah's fingers.

Even though it ended on a positive note, there was absolute silence among the five of them afterward and until they got back out onto the street. Miranda wasn't holding Noah's hand by then. She had her arm around Bruce, who looked like his eyes might pop out of his head.

"Alfred Hitchcock is a very, very bad man," he said.

Miranda insisted that they walk him home, and take Rosie too, though Walker Jones claimed he would be fine on his own. Noah doubted that, could tell by the look in his eyes too. He figured Walk would likely run home the second he was out of sight.

Once the other three were gone, Miranda and Noah walked slowly together toward her house in the cool night, snuggled in to each other again, this time for warmth. She smiled at him and whispered, "This is water."

"Pardon me?"

"It's just something I say, every now and then."

"Oh." It seemed like a private thing that he shouldn't ask her about, at least not yet.

"I'm not exactly sure what I like about that movie, other than the thrill of it," she said.

"It scared the hell out of me, but partly because it was so good."

"I know. I think, maybe, the story is about the way we are all looking at others through our own rear windows, peering out with binoculars, suspicious of everyone, putting our spin on everything. Everything out there is scary. That main character was so into himself that he nearly got his girlfriend murdered … while he watched. It's like this film is telling you a truth that scares you as much as the action does."

Noah stopped her and turned her toward him.

"I want you to be my girlfriend," he said.

"Okay," she said quietly, her eyes moistening the way they had when their faces had been a few inches apart. They stopped and held each other for five minutes or more, not caring if anyone saw them.

This is love, thought Noah, and he could not believe it. He had not felt this, nothing like this, from anyone, ever.

THEIR NEXT DATE WAS the following weekend. They took the fast train into the city to go to the art gallery. The trip took about an hour, so they had lots of time to talk on the way. They didn't once look at their phones.

"I'm not a very political person," she said at one point.

"Neither am I."

"Not that I don't follow politics. It's important that you know the issues. Especially, I think, for women."

"You sound like Constance."

"I like her. She's more than she seems."

"Aren't we all?"

"Yes, we are."

"Rosie is great too."

"She has a crush on you, has from the moment she saw you, and has had it bad since the first time she heard you say anything."

"Rosie?"

Miranda looked a little guilty. "Don't tell her I said that. Don't ever tell her. Sometimes I just say what's in my head. Man, though, you guys are blind."[26]

"What's the deal with her?"

"Do you mean, what sort of person is she?"

Noah blushed. "Yeah, that's what I meant."

"She's nice."

"That doesn't sound like a big compliment."

"I think it is."

They talked about the musicians they liked. Miranda admired lots of older music too, mixed in with new. So did Noah, another thing they had in common. She had mostly obscure

---

26 Constance told me, much later on, that girls never tell guys which girls have crushes on them, unless a girl asks them to. Apparently, it's a bit of a betrayal. Amazing the rules girls have! Miranda actually looked more than "a little guilty" when she said this. I think she was just feeling great about us, trying to flatter me, and then realized her mistake. She did say it, though.

tastes, though some were popular as well: Dylan, Haim, Lorde, Nick Cave, Phoebe Bridgers, Captain Beefheart, and Talking Heads. She liked soul and R&B too: Leon Bridges, James Brown, Etta James, Janelle Monáe, H.E.R., and Amy Winehouse. She also liked the punks, the real, original ones and new ones with an edge, like The Sex Pistols, Death Grips, Cleopatrick, PUP, Siouxsie and the Banshees, and an obscure band called Teenage Head. She didn't like the violence associated with some of them, she made that clear, or some of the lyrics, but she liked the honesty, the edginess — what she called the "authenticity."

This, thought Noah, *is the coolest person on earth.*

They also talked, of course, about books. It was difficult for Noah to keep up, but he did his best, exaggerating his knowledge, hoping it didn't show, astounded at what she had read and what she knew.[27] He was relieved to discover that he was aware of some of the novels, at least enough of them, and had what appeared to be interesting comments to make. Miranda started talking fast during this part of their conversation, almost as if her brain, her mind, had too many things to say, as if there were a lineup of subjects that she needed to talk about. It amazed him that he was the one to whom she had chosen to say these things, to whom she was unloading her pent-up thoughts.

"My mother has a hard time getting me to stop reading, actually," she said. "Though, it's kind of her fault. She is more than a little into literature, but she says that sometimes she

---

27 More about that later.

thinks I top even her. She is always after me to put out my light at night and stop reading. When I was young, she banned books from my room after bedtime, and to this day, I'm not allowed to have a lamp on my bedside table."

It was exciting to be in the city with her, just the two of them. Many of their friends back in town were almost afraid of being on its busy, colorful streets, thought it dangerous, rarely went there unless with their parents, and always for some big event. Noah and Miranda just didn't get that. He wore his thin black coat, gloveless and hatless, his brown hair sometimes in his eyes, she a thick warm navy-blue pea coat, a purple scarf wrapped around her neck in that careless yet perfect way girls somehow manage, a tight teal toque, and baby-blue woolen mittens that looked a size too large. They took the subway from the city's train station, an old one with a ceiling like a sort of working-class Sistine Chapel that they both stared up at in awe. They noticed how their voices echoed in the remarkable room, bouncing off the distant vaulted ceiling.

"I love ...," she began, staring up, her last word repeating three times after it left her lips.

"You," he answered, when her word began to die.

They looked down and grinned at each other.

"I love ...," he offered up to the ceiling.

"You," she answered, but this time, gazed right at him.

They liked the same artists too. The Group of Seven room made them sit down and stare, the van Gogh paintings, the big Seurat, the Frida Kahlo, the Georgia O'Keeffes, and a double whammy of Dali had them pulling each other from one to the next. The Warhols made them smile, so did the one Yoko

Ono. The abstract stuff left them both with questions, though Miranda had some good ideas about why Jackson Pollock's works, which looked to Noah like the artist had simply spilled his paint, might be great works of art. It had to do with the paintings being "real": honest acts of emotion put right onto the canvas, instead of pretending to make pictures that were imitations of life.

They came home on the train, hardly saying a word, she leaning on his shoulder, then he leaning on her.

"This is water," he heard her whisper again.

5
First Trouble

NOAH WAS CAREFUL ABOUT being seen any time he left the apartment to go to work. It wasn't that he didn't want anyone to know that he had a job. Lots of kids had them. In fact, having a job was a sign of being grown-up in one of the few ways that it was good to be thought of as an older person. It was just that he didn't want to do any explaining. He didn't want to lie. He didn't want to tell anyone that he was working because he was supporting his family ... his family being him and his dad. The government checks his father got didn't cover much. Neither did the fifteen hours Noah worked at the grocery store, if the truth were told. They would likely have to move again. He especially didn't want to tell Miranda anything.

"I don't know how long I can keep this from her," he whispered to himself as he held his hands in his pockets and clutched his arms to his side in his thin coat. The wind was blowing in the icy way it sometimes did in these parts in November, when it blew right into you. "Miranda Owens deserves more in a boyfriend than what she gets in me. I suppose Walk deserves more honesty from a friend too."

He kept his head down, hood on, as he strode through his neighborhood's east end. It seemed like all the bad areas in every town were in the east end. Even in the Charles Dickens novels set in London in the nineteenth century, everyone feared that part of the city. His apartment building was probably the tallest in town, seven stories high. Most of the other structures in this area were government-subsidized housing, many the same color, barely even brown. There were crack dealers around here too, though not whole gangs of them like there had been in his part of the big city, where he often had to run to or from school, or at least chose to.

"Imagine if Miranda knew I had to do that."

There was a house or two here though that had all the telltale signs: late night visitors, drapes often closed, not much furniture evident the few times you could see inside the windows.

The buildings became more commercial and he could see the grocery store up ahead.

"Me in the frozen meat department ... with a vegetarian girlfriend. Imagine if she knew that too."

Being in that department was a good thing though, in a way, because he was almost always out of sight. Any time he had to go out into the main part of the store, leave the area where he worked behind the scenes and possibly encounter customers,

he could do so surreptitiously.[28] He always peeked his head
out the swinging flap of a door first, checked out the aisles for
anyone he knew before going out, and then kept his head down
as he turned toward the meat. Customers didn't often ask him
questions. He tried to keep his bloody apron on as much as
possible, figured that warded off some people. It was one of
those stores built to look like a warehouse, giving the impression that all the produce inside was the cheapest in town.

"Fits me," he said inside his head as he went through the
front doors.

Miranda Owens was standing right in front of him, almost
blocking his way as she picked up a shopping basket. *What a
sight*, he thought, in about a million ways.

"Noah!" she cried. She dropped the basket on the floor and
threw her arms around him and he was instantly warm for the
first time since he left home. Being in her arms always felt like
home to him, the most like home anything had ever felt. It also
made him feel as if he were just visiting, since Miranda Owens
was simply too good for him. He wondered when she would
figure that out.

"What are you doing here?" she asked.

He didn't say anything.

"Noah?"

"Um ... picking something up, but you know what? I also
just realized that we have it ... stupidly ... and ... I've got to
go, got to get home."

"Who is *we*? You know you never —"

---

28 Good word for this, not just trying to impress.

"Sorry, Mir, I have to run."

With that, he turned and rushed out through the doors. As he moved along the front of the store from the outside, he eyed her peripherally through the big windows, making it seem like he was looking straight ahead. She stood still for a while, watching after him, then shrugged and turned back to her groceries. When he reached the far end of the store, he could see her through the big floor-to-ceiling windows as she headed up the aisle at the other end and turned her attention to picking the vegetables she was going to buy. She was at the opposite side of the store from the meat section. Her back was to him and then she moved out of sight. He quickly turned around, re-entered the store, slipped along the front of the row of cashiers, darted past the last one and in seconds was up the far aisle and safely through those heavy, swinging doors into the behind-the-scenes frozen meat area where he worked.

"You're late, Greene," said his boss, a heavy-set man with a square nose, flat at the front. There were faded streaks of red across his white apron, which it seemed like he had been wearing since the day he started working here more than twenty years ago.

"Yes, Mr. Swain, sorry, only a few minutes, though."

"Few minutes or fifty minutes, doesn't matter; being on time counts for something in this world."

"Yes, sir." What Noah felt like saying was that if being on time mattered so much, literally to the minute, and Mr. Swain had always been that punctual, then why was he still the manager of a frozen meat section in a grocery store in a small town?

"I have lots for you to do," said Swain. "Take the pork chops and the hams out first. Why don't you wear a warmer coat back here?"

"I'm fine, sir."

The meat was packaged and lined up and ready for him to load onto a cart and put on display. That was a problem, a big one — Miranda was still out there.

"I ... I have to use the bathroom."

"Make it quick."

He didn't. When he came back, thank God, Mr. Swain wasn't around. Noah stood by the cart for the longest time, looking at his watch, thinking about how long Miranda would be in the store, wondering how long he could chance standing here doing nothing before Swain-Swine caught him. He could not afford to lose this job.

After about ten minutes, he got sloppy. He turned his head away from the back office door, where Swain would re-enter.

"HEY!"

Noah swung around.

Swain was glaring at him. "I thought I told you —"

"Had to go back to the bathroom, a couple of times. Not feeling the best."

"What are we talking about here, a stomach issue or —"

"Yes."

"Oh." Swain paused for a moment. "Maybe you should go home."

"No. I'll be fine. I'm feeling a little better, just had to, you know, go there a few times and I —"

"Yes, you don't need to explain." He glanced at the cartload of meat. "Have you, uh, washed your hands thoroughly?"

"Yes … pretty well." Noah still didn't have his rubber gloves on.

"Pretty well?" A look of slight panic came over Mr. Swain's face. "Have you touched the meat?" He didn't wait for Noah to answer. "Go back and wash again, VERY thoroughly."

"Yes, sir."

Noah smiled as he made his way back to the bathroom. He spent as much time in there as he assumed one would spend if washing very, very, very thoroughly. By the time he came out, there was no way that Miranda could still be in the store. He seized the cart, smiled at Mr. Swain, and rushed the meat out through the heavy swinging door … and almost collided with Miranda again.

"Noah!"

At this point, he realized that all sorts of things were against him. It would now not only be obvious to her that he had lied when he last saw her, he was also doing something that he had kept hidden from her for a while … and he had almost pushed a cart full of meat into his vegetarian girlfriend.

His opening line was brilliant. "What are you doing here?"

"Me?" she said as a look that would be best described as shock came over her face. *It would have been preferable*, he thought, *if she had just been angry, but she looked upset, deeply disappointed … in him.* "I …," she began, "I forgot something and had to come back." It was impressive, actually; she was almost giving him an excuse. Maybe this was what someone who really loves you does? Then her face nearly crumpled. "Noah, what's going on?"

It was time for his face to fall. He was tough. He had been through a great deal. This, however, was unbearable. Miranda could not be lost. She just could not be lost.

"I ... I work here. I didn't tell you because it embarrasses me. I live with my father, just him, and we do not have very much. I didn't want to tell you that either, any of this." His eyes began to fill with tears. Never, even on nights when his father had come home drunk and there had been nothing to eat, had he ever cried. This was no tactic though, no calculated thing to impress this girl. He was really about to cry. It was panic time.

Miranda reached out and put a hand on his arm right where it was dangling at his side next to a bloodstain. "I love you," she said, "just the way you are."

Somehow, he had impressed her ... again. He also had the feeling, though, that impressing Miranda Owens was different than impressing other girls. There was something damn near perfect about her.

And maybe about the two of them too.

6

Home Visit

THE RELIEF NOAH FELT was enormous. Not only could he stop hiding his job from Miranda, but the release of his secret had drawn them even closer, if that was possible, and now, at least for a while, he didn't need to tell her anything else; he didn't need to explain exactly why he and his father were struggling.

He realized though, that she hadn't told him much about her parents either. In fact, after a month of dating, she had basically said nothing, and the closest he had been to her home was that night she kissed him on her veranda. He remembered the beautiful old house, the love-seat swing, the comfortable straw chairs outside on the wide, varnished boards, the glow inside, and the classy neighborhood. Miranda didn't seem like the type to hide things though. He assumed that an

opportunity just hadn't arisen, or that Miranda, smart and
cautious, was waiting for the right time to introduce him. The
fact that it was taking so long, though, worried him a little.

Sometimes she seemed like a difficult girl to date. She was
busy, beyond busy. It was almost as if their dates were things
that had to be fitted into her schedule. But he couldn't say
anything, and not only because he didn't want to blow things
between them, but because what she was doing on any given
day was always an activity about which he couldn't complain.
She, of course, set aside a great deal of time for studying, and
there were basketball games and practices, but somehow, she
also found time to do other things, for other people. She didn't
like talking about it, so sometimes he had to ask her what she
was doing when he wasn't around. The things she kept from
him seemed so much better than what he kept from her. Or
were they?

"Where were you last night?" he asked her, the day after she
had discovered his secret at the grocery store.[29] He had been
excited to see her that morning and stood waiting at the front
door of their school, the old entrance in their ancient brick
building, where the arched door still had the word GIRLS over
it, etched into the sandstone.

"Nowhere," she said and rushed by him. "I'm late."

"I called you." His heart had begun to pound. In fact, he
had been a little terrified all night and into the morning. He had

---

29 I think it was then, not always aware of exact dates in our time together.
Miranda would know, says guys always get these things wrong. She used
to tease me about this sort of thing.

called her to talk more, still reeling from what happened at the
store, still a bit insecure about it, seeking more comfort, but
her cellphone had rung and rung and rung. And she hadn't
answered two texts either. What was she doing? Was she with
another guy?

"See you later!" she cried over her shoulder, smiling at him,
but the smile seemed a little forced. He froze in place, not bothering to try to follow her.

"I thought so," he whispered to himself. She disappeared up
the stairs and out of sight. "She doesn't even want to speak
with me. This whole thing, this whole relationship, was a
fantasy."

"Hey ... bozo!"

Noah had been looking down at his shoes. Constance Mark
was standing right next to him. He hadn't seen her approach.
She was likely in tow with Miranda and he hadn't even noticed.
She had caught him rolling his eyes at her opinions once or
twice in the past and was likely glad that Miranda had left him.
She had obviously stopped to make fun of him.

He straightened up. "Go away, Constance."

"You were talking to yourself."

"You wouldn't understand."

"Actually, I think I would." She looked up the stairs where
Miranda had vanished. "Don't get possessive, Noah." Constance
started to walk past and then turned back. "She was with me,
at a seniors' home, just talking to people. She makes Rosie do
it too, at least once a week. The people there get lonely, you
know. Don't tell her I told you."

"TAKE ME WITH YOU, next time," he told Miranda as they walked out of the same entrance at the end of the day. She had smiled at him, a real smile, and taken his hand.

"Where?"

"Wherever you went last night."

She regarded him for a moment. "People aren't supposed to know. It isn't the same if people know. It means you are doing it to get praise or something. That's the way I look at it."

"Well, bring me along next time … and I won't breathe a word."

That night, she asked him over to meet her mother. That was the way she put it, and she didn't say anything else. It was almost as if she were inviting him because she felt guilty about missing his phone call the night before.

When he arrived at the door, rather than letting him in, she stepped out onto the veranda with him and took him over to the love-seat swing.

"Just so you know, I only have one parent."

"Why didn't you tell me before?" The instant that came out of his mouth, he realized it was a mistake.

"Hmm," she said. "Interesting question." She paused. "After we meet my mom today … we are going to your house tomorrow to meet your father."

"It's … it's not a house." He said it so quietly that she didn't appear to hear.

"My mom and dad split up a long time ago, when I was little," said Miranda. It seemed like there should be more to the story, but she didn't add anything. She looked down.

"Why did they break up? They grew apart?"

"It's more complicated than that," she said, lifting her head to look at him with steel in her eyes as if she were facing him on the court. "There are two reasons. The first one isn't true, it's a lie, and the second one is hard for me to deal with."

"Tell me the first one then."

"My father hit my mother."

Noah's mouth dropped open.

"Well, maybe 'hit' isn't the right word, though that's what it seemed like happened, for many years. When Mom told me, the first time, she said they were arguing and he shoved her. She said no woman should ever have to accept even that."

"She's right. I'm sorry."

"The second reason they broke up," said Miranda, "was that she was having an affair."

"What?"

"She lied the first time."

"She did?"

"Yeah. There was never any blow, not even a shove. They split up because she'd had an 'indiscretion,' as she called it when she admitted everything to me a few years ago. She said her affair was a one-night thing, not really an affair, and she cried when she told me."

Tears gathered in Miranda's eyes. Noah took her hand and they began to rock gently in the swing.

"I hated her for a while after that. My mom is a good person. She made a mistake, and by that I don't mean the affair, I totally understood why that happened when she explained it to me, or at least over the last few years as I've thought about it.

"My father was a financial trader. He was attentive to her when they dated and during their first few years of marriage, but he didn't have a lot of time for her, or for me, after that. His money-making was everything to him. He was away a lot, not very affectionate to me, and often dismissive of Mom. He shouted at her a lot."

"My mother was lonely and depressed ... and she made a mistake. She still calls it a mistake, despite her situation. I don't think it was. I think she was right to do what she did. It's the lie she told; that was the problem for me for a long time, but as the years passed, I came to understand why she did that too. I don't agree with it, never will, but I try to put myself in her shoes. She admitted the affair to my father right away and begged his forgiveness, said she would never see the other man again, that she would quit her job as a professor — that's what Mom does — so she wouldn't be near him anymore. My father left her the minute the words came out of her mouth and he hasn't spoken to us since. There wasn't an ounce of forgiveness in his heart, no hope of any, no awareness that his actions were part of the problem. He sent money for a while, but that was it. I haven't seen him since I was three. He took out his anger on me too. My mom had to raise me alone."

"You've carried this for a long time," said Noah. "How do you do it and not be bitter at all?"

"I love her."

"What?"

"I love her more than anyone else in the world." She smiled and squeezed his hand. "Or, maybe it's a tie now."

"It must be hard to always feel that way about her, kind of complicated."

"She's taught me to be a good person, to love others no matter what. She's also taught me about what it is to be fallible, to make mistakes, and the need for forgiveness. I've learned that forgiveness is not just about the person you forgive, but about yourself too."

This is *my* girlfriend, thought Noah, feeling again like he was weightless.

"It took a lot for her to tell me the truth later on," continued Miranda. "It must have been incredibly hard. She was willing to possibly destroy my whole image of her in order to tell the truth when it had to be told. I guess the way she raised me, the values she instilled in me, allowed me not to hate her, at least after a while. She and I talk a lot about not being perfect, about the fact that the most important thing in life is not being a good person, since that's difficult to do … but trying to be one. It's the trying that matters." She dropped her voice. "This is water."

He was going to have to ask her what that meant, but now didn't seem like the time.

"Let's go in and meet my amazing mom," said Miranda quietly.

SAMANTHA OWENS WAS EVERYTHING Miranda said she was. She was a smart, happy lady who was almost a clone of her daughter, who could have almost passed for her older sister — tall, short-haired, and radiant — and she welcomed him as if he were already a part of their family.

"I've heard a great deal about you," she said, her face bright with anticipation, an expression that said, *I'm looking forward to getting to know you.*

"I hope it's all been good."

"Oh, it's good, believe me."

"No need to elaborate, Mom."

"Noah, why don't you and I sit down and I'll tell you everything she's said about you in as much detail as I can recall."

"Let's do it," said Noah.

Samantha laughed. "I like you already."

He made sure to help them finish getting dinner ready. He knew enough to do that, especially in a house run by two women. Miranda's mother seemed appreciative, smiling at him as he cut the cucumbers in his clumsy way, touching his hands as she helped him squeeze the lime onto them, and directing the amount of Himalayan Pink Salt he applied. "You know," she said quietly at one point, "Miranda acts like she's strong, but she's wanted someone, wanted a guy, to be honest, who gets her, for a long time." Samantha didn't say anything else, didn't say that guy was him, but she made eye contact when she said it. She had put some sort of jazz on and it wafted gently through the beautiful, elegant old house as if it were coming naturally out of the walls. The place felt warm and friendly, though a little like it was from another time. The furniture seemed Victorian to him, though he wasn't sure, and it contrasted with the mostly modern art and sculptures that were perfectly placed on the walls and coffee tables. It was all so different from any home he had ever had. He and Miranda kept exchanging secret smiles.

"I hear you like to read," said Samantha once they had all sat down to eat. It was linguine with pesto, sun-dried tomatoes, and some sort of old cheese, and it smelled great.[30]

"He's got exceptional taste."

"So, what are you reading?"

He had noticed her office at the top of the stairs, the door wide open, the room lined with books. There were also bookshelves packed with impressive volumes in the living room. He noticed Alice Munro, Michael Ondaatje, Emma Donoghue, Thomas King, and Yann Martel. It wasn't only novels for adults either. He saw lots of kids' and teen literature too: picture books by Robert Munsch, novels by Walters and Peacock and Martha Brooks, and sets of John Green stories, *Looking for Alaska* sticking out as if it had just been read. Miranda hadn't said exactly what Samantha taught, but he was getting the feeling, quickly, that it was literature of some sort, that her specialty was perhaps Victorian, maybe modern, perhaps YA, maybe some sort of interesting combination of all of that.

"Uh ... we just studied Shakespeare's *King Lear*."

"She knows who wrote it, Noah."

"No, that's okay, Mir. It's great to hear that name come out of a young person's mouth, especially without a sneer. What else?"

"Well, we're studying early modern texts, so we've looked at Woolf and Hemingway, Colette, and some simpler Joyce and —"

"That sounds excellent. Miranda and I have had many great discussions about everything she's read in that course."

---

30 I think that's what it was — not up on all the Italian pastas.

"Arguments too," said Miranda, looking at the pasta as she twirled it on her fork.

"Yes, we've disagreed quite a few times, but that's good. Actually though, Noah, I didn't mean to ask about what you are studying. I meant what are you reading at home, for fun? That says something about your interests."

Noah felt his heart picking up its pace. He was sure that he was a fake at many things in life — he had to be to survive — but perhaps especially about this. Yes, he liked some of the books he was studying; he had some ability to decipher them, and he definitely liked the fact that Miranda was impressed with his interest in reading them and his sensitivity and level of understanding about them and the marks he was getting ... but he was harboring some secrets. He rarely read the books all the way through. He latched on to things that he understood, on to themes and meanings, then skimmed the rest of the books so he wouldn't disappoint his brilliant girlfriend. Sometimes, he even looked up the plots online. He never read anything away from school. He didn't have time. He had to work, look after his father. He had to worry. What was he going to say to Miranda's mother? Perhaps the truth would do? No. That wasn't even remotely affordable. He thought of the names of some of the authors that Miranda had mentioned recently, the ones she seemed to most admire, and picked one.

"Um ... I'm reading David Foster Wallace."

Samantha paused for a moment. "Really? That's impressive, very impressive. I would doubt that any other student in your grade is reading his work. You know, you've chosen just about the most complicated author one can imagine." Then she narrowed her eyes. "He has quite a reputation, an interesting one. You aren't one of those boys who says they are reading Wallace only to impress the girls, are you?"

Noah didn't know what to say. His heart was pounding now. He had lied to Miranda's mother. He didn't even know the name of a single David Foster Wallace book.

"Mom," said Miranda curtly.

Samantha turned to her. "Shouldn't pursue this?" She turned back to Noah. "Mir and I have some disagreements about Wallace. I think he is a mostly-for-males sort of writer, and he wasn't always the best person, to say the least. Miranda doesn't care about any of that."

"I care, Mom."

Then they started arguing. Noah didn't even bother to follow it. All he caught was that they both agreed that this author was brilliant, astonishingly so, but that other factors made falling completely for him problematic. Miranda kept saying that he "told the truth about life, about himself, about guys." There was also that thing about smart boys finding out that his work was apparently genius and complicated and pretending they had read some of it to impress girls … exactly what Noah had just done. Many of these twits apparently kept a long novel Wallace wrote called *Infinite Jest* on their bookshelves, prominently displayed, and went on and on about it to girls. Apparently, there was even lots online about this very thing. The only good thing about this Miranda-Samantha debate was that they had completely forgotten to ask him more about which book he was actually reading. He would not have had an answer — this *Infinite Jest* thing with all its complexities would have been a risky choice. He would have had to have guessed about something general he could say about it and then rush out and buy it, and it likely cost a boatload, and then read the whole bloody thing for the next time he saw either of them — and the two of them, together, would probably have caught him in a lie anyway. Right away. That might have spelled the end for him and Miranda.

His girlfriend, though, surprised him again.

As he was leaving that night, stepping out onto the porch with her after receiving a warm hug from Samantha, she turned him toward her, her hands on his shoulders to make him look her in the eye.

"You haven't read any Wallace, have you?"

"No," he said without a pause. He couldn't lie to her up this close. This was it. Game over.

"That's okay," she said.

"What?"

"It was endearing, actually, you trying to impress Mom and me. Took some balls."

"Thanks, I think."

"Just don't lie to me again, or to my mom, okay? I'm not good with lies, as you know. Small lies can beget big ones, make you do other bad things too, I think. I don't know if I would be able to forgive another important person in my life for doing something bad to me again."

"Okay."

"Let's be honest with each other, all right? Really honest, all the time?"

He hoped she couldn't see him gulp. How could he be completely honest with her? How could he not? He was hoping she
had forgotten about wanting to come to his house tomorrow.

"Okay," he said again.

She smiled at him and rested her forehead against his. They
were silent for a few seconds. Noah wished it would go on
forever. *This*, he thought, *is what heaven would feel like.*

"I'll be back in a second," she said, turned and slipped inside
the house. He could hear her going up the stairs. He considered
where she was headed. To her bedroom. He imagined that, what
it would look like. Miranda Owens' bed.[31] He shook his head
and paced on the veranda. In less than a minute she was back.
She had a small book in her hand.

"This is one of Wallace's. He wrote a wide variety of things:
unbelievably good non-fiction, short stories, and two and a
half novels."

"Two and a half?"

"Didn't finish one of them, though *Infinite Jest* might as
well be three on its own. It's more than a thousand pages long,
including footnotes."

"A THOUSAND pages? Footnotes? I thought it was a novel."

"It is. You should try to read all of it, if you can, because it's
worthwhile. I think you are up to it. I've read it twice." She
laughed. "Now I'm in the boy role, trying to impress you."
She paused. "Wallace was a jerk at times, Mom is right, and
maybe that's not even a strong enough word. Sometimes, from
reading him, I think that he knew it though, or at least even-

---

31 Sorry.

tually figured it out, wanted to try to do better as a man and a human being, wanted himself and others at least to attempt to change our basic natures, our default positions, which are always self-concerned and self-gratifying."

"I thought he was a very modern writer, a current guy, but you keep talking about him in the past tense, as if he's dead."

"He is. Suicide."

"Oh ..." Noah looked down at the little book in her hand. "What's that?"

"It's one of his works, very short. Something he wrote in his later days. It's for you. I love you, Noah."

He looked down at the title as she passed it into his hand.

This Is Water.

7
Another Home

MIRANDA HADN'T FORGOTTEN.

In fact, she had it all planned out in detail. Noah was to meet her at her house — since he had said that he didn't live too far away — and they would walk to his place. When he arrived, she was carrying her backpack.

"What's that for?"

"A little surprise for your dad."

They walked for a while in silence, his eyes cast downward. It was a cold November night. She was bundled up in her parka, the hood pulled around her face. Her long nose was red within minutes, but she didn't complain. Her boots and his shoes crunched in the snow. He was thinking about how he had tried to deceive her at her house last night, the fact that he had lied to her a couple of times already and what that might mean for their future, sweating under his thin coat.

"You and I are going to go out and buy you a new —"

"Miranda," he said forcefully, cutting her off in mid thought.

She stopped suddenly and looked at him. He could tell that his tone had scared her. His worry was on his face too. He felt vulnerable. He hadn't been able to sleep last night. Though a relationship with Miranda Owens seemed like a dream come true, he wondered now if its inevitable end might destroy him, be so bad that it wouldn't be worth the joy it had given him so far. He was going to mess up, again. How would he ever recover when she had enough and rejected him? He would look and feel weak. He couldn't afford that. Perhaps the safest way, the way to protect himself, was to end it now, before there was no turning back. Do it himself, be strong.

"Yes?" she said quietly.

"I'm not sure this is working." He felt faint and could barely say it.

"What ... what do you mean by ... this?"

"Us."

"Noah ... what do you mean? I ... I thought ..." He had never heard Miranda Owens' voice sound shaky. In a way, it was flattering.

"I keep lying to you."

"Lying?" She smiled. "Oh, don't worry about your job. I get why you kept it a secret, and I get why you didn't tell the truth about the Wallace book either. I —"

"We don't live nearby. It will take us about half an hour to get there. It's in the east end of town, the far east end."

"Oh." She started walking again and he moved with her to keep up. "Well, that's not surprising," she added. "I figured you didn't live in a palace when I found out about your job. I didn't tell you much about Mom and our relationship before you met her either." He couldn't believe it — she was making excuses for him, again.

"Yeah. We're funny about that, you and I. We talk so much, but in some ways, we don't say a lot."

"Actually, I think we say a great deal. We just had a few things that were private for us, that we had a hard time sharing." She looked at him hopefully. "But we are now." She slid her arm through his and snuggled into him. "This is working, believe me." She squeezed him as if she wouldn't let go.

He had always wondered if he was actually in love with her. After all, he had never experienced anything that anyone would call true love in a relationship before. He hadn't ever had a serious girlfriend. He had shied away from that. He couldn't remember his mother's embrace or even her face. His father had certainly never told him that he loved him or even touched him, other than the odd drunken slap on the back. He was in love now, though. He knew it.

He also knew that he could never cross her again.

"Let's stop talking nonsense," she said, looking away from him, obviously hoping he wouldn't pursue this discussion anymore. "Did you read the little book I gave you?"

Here was another opportunity to lie to her. He couldn't, though.

"I started it."

"Started it? Noah, it's barely a hundred pages long. Short ones."

He had made a go at it, read the first ten pages or so: a

curious opening about a couple of fish who did not realize that they were living in water. The whole book was a commencement address that Wallace had given at a college,[32] one of those things where an important person tells students all about life and what they should think. It wasn't promising. He had actually been disappointed that Miranda thought this thing was so important.

"Haven't had time."

"You don't have to read it. I just thought you might like it." She didn't let go of him as she said this, squeezed his hand, in fact. They walked on for a while.

"I have to prepare you for what you are going to see at my place," said Noah.

"A man cave? A boy's unkempt abode? I think I can handle it."

"It's more than that. We live in an apartment and my father doesn't do anything."

"What do you mean?"

"He hasn't worked for a long time, since even before my mom died, when I was little. I don't remember her. I have a sister, had one, Mary Jane, she's about six years older than me. She left quite a few years ago. She lives on the west coast. She texts me sometimes. My father lives off Workers' Compensation. He claims he hurt his back at work on a construction site long ago. I guess he did. His doctor was an old friend. He gets around okay now, plays up his pain and all the medication he's on when he has to get a check-up or see a compensation

---

32 Found out it was Kenyon College, in Gambier, Ohio, May 21, 2005.

official. His checks are small, though. He is growing more and more paranoid that people are watching him, so he only goes out when he has to, and stays in his room a lot. We usually end up not being able to meet our rent and we do a lot of moving. That's why we came here. That's why I have to work. He spends a fair bit of what he makes on online things. He drinks a lot ... I'm kind of his parent."

It all came out in a torrent. They kept walking for a while after that in silence.

"Okay," Miranda finally said. That was all she said, but it made Noah Greene feel ten feet tall.

Her face didn't change at all when she saw his apartment building or when they got into the smelly lobby or when the elevator groaned and shrugged before it began a noisy, bouncy ride up to his floor. In fact, she held him even tighter. They leaned against each other and against the wall as they rose. Then, he unconsciously let out a sigh and paused for a moment as they stood on the bare carpet outside his door. He unlocked it and put his finger to his lips to let her know to keep quiet. The door creaked. They went in.

The whole place was dim, with no lights on in the narrow rectangular room that served as a living room and dining room, or in the small kitchen. Noah guided them away from the short hallway on their left that appeared to lead down to a couple of closed doors. It was now evident that the bit of light that at least made the few items of furniture visible was coming from under a door down there. Noah hoped she didn't notice that there wasn't a book in sight. They moved toward one of the couches. The window that looked out over the subsidized housing in the east end of town had dirty streaks on it, as if someone had attempted to clean it,[33] but hadn't known how to do it effectively. Noah clicked on a lamp and the contents of the room became clearer. Miranda sat on the black leather couch with a little crunch, her jeans catching on a rip in the surface. She looked across at the two mismatched chairs against the opposite wall, one sort of yellow, the other green, and the old tube television in the corner near the window. Noah didn't offer to take her coat. He sat down beside her.

"I think we have some milk or something. Would you like a drink?" he asked quietly.

"I'm okay." She set her backpack down on the floor since there wasn't a table in the room. She looked over and saw a counter between this room and the little kitchen, the place where they ate. Noah stood up.

"What are we going to do?" asked Miranda.

"Pardon me?"

"I thought we were eating. Aren't we going to eat with your father?"

Noah paused for a second. "No." He paused again, unsure if he should go to the kitchen to get himself something to drink or say something more. "I don't think that would be wise. I thought ... I thought ... I'd simply show you the place, like you asked, and then we could walk back to your house."

"Have you eaten?"

"... uh ..."

"Noah."

---

33 That would be me.

"No. That's all right, though. I'll eat later."

"Sit beside me again."

He sat.

"I have some banana bread muffins in this backpack. I made them. That is not a small thing, my dear. I am no cook, believe me. If you want someone like that, then you are barking up the wrong tree." He couldn't bring himself to smile. "I made them for your dad, really. If you think that after sweating my butt off trying to make some at least half-decent muffins for you guys, I am going to just deposit them here and head out, you have another thing coming. Where's your dad?" She steeled her face. "I want to meet him. I want to eat a muffin or two with him."

There was a noise in the hall, a door shoved open and a form appeared through the opening in the wall between the old television and the chairs. Someone was staggering forward. He was naked.

"Dad!" cried Noah, leaping to his feet. Miranda turned away.

Noah got between them and steered his father back toward his room.

"I have to piss!" His father slurred.

"There's someone here."

"What?"

"There's someone here. A friend of mine."

"Well, then I'll meet him. Where is he?"

"She."

"A girl? You've got a girl here, boy? Now we're talkin'! Let's have a look!"

"Not yet," said Noah. "This way, Dad." He turned his father and steered him back into his bedroom. After the door closed, there were a few shouts and then it got quieter. After a while, the door opened again and the two of them came out and walked into the living room/dining room.

"This is my father, Robert Greene. Dad, this is Miranda."

The man looked old enough to be Noah's grandfather. He may have once been his son's height, but now walked with a stoop. His thick brown and white hair had been combed roughly and unevenly, as if someone else had done it [34] and his eyes were bloodshot. He was wearing pajamas, in bare feet, and smelled of alcohol.

"Well, it is my pleasure, Miss …?"

"Owens," said Miranda, rising to her feet and giving him a smile that appeared to melt him. She took his hand.

"My, my," he said. "You are a fine one."

"Well, now you've met," said Noah, looking forlorn and trying to pull his father away. Robert Greene had a firm grip on Miranda's hand.

"Wait," she said, somehow loosening his hold without seeming rude and reaching down to pick up her backpack. "I brought you something." When she looked back up to his old, lined face, he was glancing toward his son. "No, I mean for you, Mr. Greene."

"For me?" he slurred.

"Of course." She smiled.

She patted the seat next to her. Noah reluctantly released him

---

34 That would be me.

and the three of them sat. Then they feasted on the muffins, his father sitting in the middle. They didn't say much. Mr. Greene ate loudly and with great satisfaction. He answered her brief questions with mostly one-word answers, his focus on the food. After he had consumed four muffins, Noah got him to his feet again.

"Time for bed, Dad."

As Robert Greene allowed himself be led toward his bedroom, he said over his shoulder, "It's been a slice." He almost tripped as he approached the hallway and Miranda noticed that Noah then took him by the hand. She heard them enter the bathroom, the toilet seat come up, someone urinating. "Wash," said Noah, his instruction audible through the closed door, and she heard water running. "Here," she heard Noah say next and then the sound of someone brushing his teeth. Then they loped down the hallway again, Noah supporting his father again. They were inside the bedroom for a long time. As she listened and heard their muffled conversation, she realized that Noah was actually putting his father in bed. He reappeared a short while later.

"Let's go," he said, not looking at her.

Out on the street, she clung to him again and they walked to her house in silence. When they arrived, the lights were out, and when they got inside, they realized that no one was home. They went in and sat on the beautiful old white settee in the Victorian living room and both felt as if they were back in time and in a wonderful reality of their own. It may have had something to do with her mood. She was holding on to him, almost clutching him to her. They started to kiss.

Miranda had never kissed him like this. Soon, she reached under his shirt and put her hands on his bare chest, then snaked them behind his back and pulled him toward her. He could feel her strength as she held him tightly, her hands anxiously moving up and down his back. She put her leg over his hip and pulled the bottom part of her body to him too. He began to breathe heavier. He reached under her sweater. She pulled back.

"Sorry," he said.[35]

"No. Don't be sorry." She kissed him again, passionately. "I ... I wish we could. I want to. Just not yet." She kissed him again. "We will. I promise you, Noah Greene." Then she held her forehead against his.

---

35 I was sure I had made a big mistake there, could not help myself though.

8

Christmas and
an Everlasting Love

ON CHRISTMAS DAY, NOAH set up his father in front of the
television with a basket of fruit and chocolates, then headed to
the Owens' house for dinner. Miranda greeted him at the door
in a red, woolen one-piece and Santa hat that just about melted
his heart. She pulled him indoors. He was bearing her gift in
his right hand and her mother's in his left. He had gone to a
second-hand bookstore and found a Zadie Smith novel that
Miranda was sure Samantha hadn't read. The gift for his girlfriend, though, was another matter. She had told him not to
buy her anything, but he couldn't bear not getting her something. He'd carved a few dollars out of his side of the food
budget each week and frequented clothing stores he would
not normally enter and jewelers shops whose wares confused

him, doing so almost daily since the beginning of December, desperate to make the right choice. He even considered asking Rosie or Constance to help him, but word might get back to Miranda that he'd had assistance, and he wanted her to know that he had made the choice himself.

What to choose, though? He knew she would be happy with anything, even if he just gave her one of his shirts for pajamas, or something like that, maybe especially something like that, but he wanted to do better. In fact, he yearned to make a choice that would dazzle her. How could he do that with his meagre resources? Then it came to him.

"Rosie, Constance, and Bruce were by this morning," Miranda said, leading him into the warm old living room. It always seemed like something from a Dickens novel in there, from the happy part of Scrooge's life that is, or John Jarndyce's warm home,[36] with a fire on in the fireplace and now with a perfect fat tree tastefully decorated. There was only a single present under it, but it was large.

"Noah!" cried Samantha coming in from the kitchen with a platter of hot cider. "You missed the crowd this morning! I told Mir that you should have been invited too, but for some reason she wanted just you for dinner." She winked at him.

"Mom," said Miranda firmly. Samantha made a motion of zipping her lips.

Noah set his girlfriend's precious gift gently beneath the tree and turned to her mother. "This is for you," he said, handing Samantha her present.

---

36 That's from *Bleak House*. Mir and I loved that book.

"Very impressive," she said. "Get the mother a present. Good job, my boy."

She loved it, the only Zadie Smith she hadn't read. Miranda gave him a knowing smile and Samantha wrapped him up in a hug.

Then Miranda and Noah sat down for the main event.

"I'll leave you two alone," said Samantha, disappearing into the kitchen.

"You first," said Miranda the second her mother left, dropping down to her knees next to the big present and pushing it along the floor toward him.

He wondered what in the world she would get him. It would tell him something about her. He was always anxious to know more about Miranda Owens, especially when it involved her affection for him. There was a big heart drawn on the outside and the words, *Our First Christmas, I Love You* written inside, surrounded by *x*'s and *o*'s. He tried to open the present slowly, but it was hard not to move fast. He wondered if she could see that his hands were trembling. The item inside felt soft. Accidentally, as he tried to unstick a bit of scotch tape, he tore a piece of wrapping paper and saw what was beneath. It was black and nylon and he could see a marketing tag. "The Warmest Parka on the Planet," it read. He stopped instantly and dropped it. He felt tears rushing to his eyes and turned his head away. He brought his hands up to his face, fighting with everything he had not to break down. He stood up. Then he heard her slowly unwrapping the rest of the big down-filled coat and getting to her feet. She put it on him and slipped inside it with him. This time she didn't have to say that she loved him.

"You're ... you're next," he stammered, pressing her to him so she couldn't see him wipe his face.

She almost leapt from the coat and seized the gift, holding it to her chest.

"I love it."

"You haven't opened it yet."

"I love it."

"Open it, goofball."

"If you insist."

He had never seen Miranda act even remotely girlish before. That wasn't a word you would associate with her. Right now, though, she was decidedly that way, acting a bit shy, looking at the gift and back at him.

"It'd better not be naughty."

"I would never do such a thing."

"Spoilsport."

"Just open it."

"I have to read what you wrote on the outside first."

"Please do."

She read it out loud. "To Miss Miranda Owens from Mr. Noah Greene, Esquire, with Appropriate Affections on the Occasion of this Festive Season."

She laughed. Not just a little. For a while, she could not stop. "I may pee myself before I get this thing open," she was finally able to say.

"I'll do it."

She pulled it back from him and in an instant, she had it out, and gasped.

He had seen it in a department store while looking for

clothes and jewelry, a little light with bendable wires and a clip, to attach to a book so you could read at night. *For you, at night*, read the little card, *when your mother and the rest of the world, except me, want you to be asleep.* He had carved their initials on either side of a plus sign on the little plastic base.

Now *she* was crying.

Bingo, he thought.

"I just thought I would —" began Samantha as she sashayed back into the room. When she saw the two of them kneeling in front of each other and her daughter in tears, reaching out for Noah's face, she did an abrupt turn and exited like a vaudeville comedian hooked off a stage.

They didn't even notice.

"Thank you," whispered Miranda. She put her forehead against his again. "You're the one, you know, Noah; you're the one."

THE NEXT EIGHT MONTHS flew by like a dream. Everything went well. School was fun together; basketball was even better than before because they came to every one of each other's games and pushed one another to new heights. They somehow brought Constance, Walker, Rosie, and Bruce into reasonable, albeit at times strained, friendships too. Their own relationship kept thriving. They never fought, never had so much as a harsh word for each other. Miranda made muffins for Mr. Greene every week and insisted on eating them with him, Noah agreeing provided he sat between the two of them. They studied together, spending most of their time on English class homework, and often compared their high marks — Miranda's always a little better than Noah's. Mr. Mitchell told them they should both be writers. He didn't know, of course, that Noah still didn't read the assigned novels all the way through, still getting by with reading parts, looking up the rest of the plot online and using his innate ability to understand how stories worked. Even Miranda didn't catch on.

The intimate part of their relationship was the most frustrating, for both of them. They had a hard time keeping their hands off each other, and several times when they were alone — usually at Miranda's house — they almost went all the way. She was having a terrible time with what to do, not wanting to give in to her yearnings.[37] She told him she didn't know why she wanted to wait longer, but she did, and hoped he would understand. She assured him that it wouldn't be long. She wanted things to be perfect between the two of them. Though waiting was mind-bogglingly difficult, he truly did understand. Her approach was part of being Miranda, deep down he admired it and wouldn't want it any other way. He worried that he lacked class, lacked integrity, and he knew that his remarkable girlfriend was almost made of such things.

"IS NOAH A GOOD kisser?" Rosie asked Miranda deep into a "girls' night" one spring evening at the Gonzalez home, Constance examining her pants to pick off a piece of lint, as if she had no interest in the answer. Miranda knew that Rosie had wanted to ask this question for months, and that she had only

---

37 Having "a terrible time" wouldn't quite capture my own feelings about this at key moments in our intimacies. Resisting my urges with Miranda Owens was like having my eyes, or something else, burned out with hot coals.

worked up the courage to inquire, in a small voice, well into an intimate conversation about relationships with boys that night.

"Who cares?" snarled Constance.

"Yes, Rosie, he is," said Miranda and almost giggled. It was very un-Miranda-like.

It was difficult to tell if Rosie liked the answer or not.

"I hope you made the first move," said Constance. "You need to be the one in charge of the kissing."

"So, we girls should be the kissers, not the kiss-ees?" asked Miranda.

She and Rosie laughed, as Constance tried to hold back a grin.

"I could be a kiss-ee," said Rosie.

"Have some spine, Ro."

"I think we should be both," said Miranda. "That's more fun."

"You have to be careful about fun with guys."

"Have you two gone all the way?" asked Rosie suddenly. She turned beet red the second she asked the question. She hadn't intended it to come out. It had just shot from her brain, or somewhere else. There was silence for a moment. "Sorry," she added.

"No, Ro, that's okay. I think it's important that we share things and be honest with each other. Especially about these things. Keeping it inside isn't good for us."

"So?" asked Constance, drawing a circle with her finger on the pillow she was holding. "What's the answer?"

Miranda sighed. "No. No, we haven't gone all the way. I'm sure he wants to."

"No kidding."

"But so do I."

"Really?" asked Rosie.

"Of course. This is Noah, ladies. This is my guy."

"Yeah, of course."

"I think you're wise to take your time," said Constance.

"And I'm frustrated too."

Constance and Rosie waited for her to say more.

"I feel like a prude sometimes about it. Noah is really good and he never pressures me."

"He better not."

"Oh, I don't mean like that, Con. I just mean he never makes me feel like I should be doing something that I'm still not quite comfortable with."

"That's amazing."

"But I promised him we'd do it soon."

"You did?" The two girls had spoken together.

"Yeah," she said, "and I mean it." The smile that came over her face had different reactions inside the minds and bodies of Constance Mark and Rosie Gonzalez.[38]

WALKER AND NOAH NEVER talked about such intimate things. Walk was dying to know everything, of course, and if his buddy's girlfriend had been anyone other than Miranda, he might have actually inquired, probably in some sort of snide way

---

38 Rosie told me most of this, though I had to imagine some of it. Hope I got it close to right.

while they were shooting hoops or something. He knew enough though, to keep quiet about all of that. Instead, he and Noah stuck to important things like sports trivia, what was going on with the singers and bands they liked, the weird ways of celebrities and athletes, and things they could work on together from school. They didn't talk about books. Walk wasn't into it enough, and assumed Noah only talked about them to impress Miranda. After many months with this new friend and his association with Miranda and her cohorts, Walker Jones still kept his head down in life, generally. He was having a strange time dealing with Constance Mark though, and not just because he disagreed with her all the time. There was something about her he couldn't put his finger on. They argued a lot, but in a weird way. It was almost as if they both enjoyed it.

SO, ON LIFE WENT for the six of them through to the end of school and into the summer. They did nearly everything together, Miranda and Noah leading the way, a golden couple in their midst, Rosie adoring them both, Constance and Walk bickering, and Bruce desperate to be with the group whenever he could, his long factual accounts of various subjects occasionally gushing out of him, tolerated by the other five. All but Bruce found jobs that summer: Noah keeping his at the grocery store, Miranda working the front desk at the public library, and Constance and Walker somehow both at the same job greeting visitors at the tourism booth in front of city hall. They all cherished the time they had together and spent a great deal of it at the beach. It was perfect. Miranda and Noah were destined for a future together that they all imagined was more wonderful than one could expect out of life.

Until the day when it all fell apart, when Noah destroyed everything.

It was because of what he said.

9

What Noah Said

WHEN LISA ANN ENTERED the portable change room, her presence almost filled Noah with fear. Almost. He did not want her in there and dreaded the consequences if anyone knew. There was another sensation, however, that ran through him, which, if he were honest, could only be described as thrilling. Lisa Ann Bordeaux was inches from him. They were alone together. She was looking up at him. She was wearing ... well ... she was as earlier described,[39] and the truth ... the absolute truth ... was that he was enticed by her in a way that he feared he had no control over. That fact, that sensation, loomed in the little room and in his mind and throughout his body for at least a second, the longest second of his life, a second that seemed longer than his entire life, as long as male and female

---

39 See flowery little bikini, Chapter 1.

human beings had existed, a second during which he could have made a thousand decisions. Noah had to reach within himself to master the sensation, well within himself. He had to make an intellectual decision. His mind had to be rational in the face of everything else that was bombarding it.

"Hi," she said, that little word uttered softly and seductively and yet somehow sounding loud and clear above the closing of the spring door behind her. It seemed like it had a dozen syllables. Her brown eyes locked on him. It was as if she were mesmerizing him.

Then, she added more.

"I like you, you know, a lot."

Then she reached for him. He was shirtless, his hands on the top button of his jeans. In the nick of time, his mind did the right thing: his hands shot up and seized hers. The two of them, girl and boy, stood that way for a moment, holding hands, but his slightly bending hers back, pushing her away.

She gave a little gasp of pain and smiled, and then spoke calmly. "Come on, Noah," she said. "Miranda isn't here. Let's have a little fun."

"No," he blurted out.

"No?" she asked and made her eyes big. "Really?"

"No," he repeated.

"You have to live, Noah. You can't be good all the time. You can't be perfect."

Miranda Owens stood just outside the blue portable change room in the heat of the late summer day, amidst the sounds on the beach, amidst her love for Noah, their love for each other, it now dangling on the edge of a cliff. She might as well have been in the change room with them. Their conversation was that clear.

"I'm not good all the time," said Noah to Lisa Ann, "and neither is Miranda."

"Oh? I hear differently. I hear she won't —"

And that was when he said it.

Miranda knew enough not to interfere. This was up to Noah. She waited to hear what he was going to say.

"We've done it many times," he said.[40]

---

40 Though ... that isn't exactly what I said. The last two words are accurate, but I've changed the first three. ... because there's one word in there that I can't bring myself to write.

10
Descent

HOW DO YOU RECOVER from something like that?

Noah kept asking himself that question. Miranda, of course, had to recover from it too, but over the first few weeks, he never once considered that. He was far too devastated. His thoughts revolved around himself. He was irrational, crushed in a way that he never thought possible.

When she ran from him that day, after he had dropped to his knees and told her that he loved her, after he had pursued her, pleaded with her, begged her, wept in front of her, he actually felt like he was going to lose consciousness. He watched her disappear into the blocks north of the main street, fleeing from him as if he were the Devil. Once, he thought, she appeared to glance back, but then set her face the other way and vanished into her neighborhood. He leaned over, hands on knees, heaving, wishing his heart would burst and he could collapse right there. Perhaps, he thought, she would somehow hear him hit the pavement and would turn, come back, return him to life with a kiss.

None of that happened. There were just the sounds of cars slowly passing, birds singing, a light wind rustling in the trees; maybe some people looked out their windows at the crumpled boy. Life was going forward. Without him. Without them.

It had all happened so suddenly. Everything he desired had been there in the palm of his hand, right there in his secure grasp for nearly eleven months. Now it was gone, like the fairy tale it had always been.

He walked back to his apartment. No one picked up his trail and followed him. How could they? He had never even told Walk where he lived. Only Miranda knew.

He didn't go out for the next few days, hoping that Miranda would appear. He sat on the torn old black leather sofa for hours at a time, ignoring his father, who barely seemed to notice that he was constantly in the apartment. Every second, whether lying awake in bed or back on the sofa, Noah was perpetually thrilled and terrified by the idea that a call from her might ring on his phone, or a buzz would sound on their intercom, or a knock would come on his door. He jumped at any noise and his heart beat much faster than it should. He didn't answer Walk's many calls and texts or the one from Rosie. His thoughts spiraled in dangerous circles, considering if there was anything worth living for now. Not once during those few days did he think of Miranda's pain. There was still too much of his own.

Somehow, when Wednesday night came, a week and a half

from the start of school, he got himself off the sofa and down the street to work.

"If your lip was any further out," said Mr. Swain the minute he saw him, "you'd be a duck."[41]

"Sorry."

"What? Speak up."

"Sorry, having a bad day."

"Look, kid, we all have bad days, but don't bring it in here. We've got a job to do." He wiped his blue-rubber glove on his stained white apron, adding another smudge of red.

Swain-Swine had no idea.

"I've had my troubles too," he continued, snapping his thick, ring-less fingers, as thick as the bloody ribs he chopped, out of one of the gloves.

Not like this, thought Noah.

"You don't see me advertising them, though. Toughness, my friend, is what gets you through hard times." Swain shoved a big cart forward, his bull's shoulders driving the wheeled steel vehicle clean across the room to Noah. "Get this stuff out onto the shelves."

I should tell him to go screw himself, thought Noah, *but what's the point of saying anything, doing anything, of going on?*

"Forgot one!" Swain yelled, and when Noah looked toward him, he saw a head-less, beak-less, feather-less, claw-less chicken, plump and butchered to its white skin, flying through the air toward him, heading in an arc into the cart. A streak of

---

41 "And you resemble one of these pigs you are packaging," I felt like saying, but I held that in.

blood flew from it like a thread of Jackson Pollock paint and he could feel a tiny bit splat against his cheek as the dead bird landed with a plop in a perfect hit in the cart.

"Three points!" yelled Swine.

Miranda was right about her choice of food, thought Noah, as he wiped the blood from his face. She was right about everything. She was right about me.

ABOUT THREE-QUARTERS OF the way through getting the meat into its proper places, purposely misplacing some of it to piss off Swain, he noticed that someone was standing right next to him. He kept his back to whomever it was, but the figure still didn't move. He glanced down and saw a pair of running shoes, black-and-white, and the cuffs of pink jeans. He knew who it was.

"Hi, Noah," she said quietly.

He looked at her. "Rosie."

"Do you want to talk?" Her voice was barely audible. She sounded awfully nervous and was clutching her cell in both hands.

"No."

"I think it would be better if —"

"Look, Miranda's right. I'm a piece of shit, okay?"

He was a little shocked to see that her eyes were red. He couldn't tell if she was sad, though, or what it was. It seemed like a mass of emotions were moiling on the other side of those black eyes.

"Oh … I don't think you should call yourself —"

"No, Rosie, I'm a piece of crap. I'm an imposter too, always have been. I'd be better off dead. You and everyone you know would be better off steering clear of me."

"I'm not going to do that."

"I lied to another girl about Miranda, a girl I don't even care about, to impress her. I told her I'd had SEX WITH MIRANDA, okay?"

And he didn't even add exactly how he had put it. But he said it loudly. Not only did Rosie's eyes grow wide, but several customers in the aisle stopped and turned toward them. It was only at that instant that Noah realized that someone else had overheard them too, standing near the swinging door to the freezer room at the back of the store.

Swain.

"Mr. Greene!" he said clearly. He might as well have said it over a loudspeaker. "Please be good enough to step back here for a moment."

"Maybe you are a piece of shit," he heard Rosie say quietly.

It hurt to hear her say that. "I've got to go," Noah muttered, and he turned and pushed his cart toward Swain.

"I'll wait for you outside," he heard her say.

He sighed and turned back to her for a moment. "Rosie, don't do that. Swain is either going to fire me, which will put me in an even worse mood, or you'll have to wait until the end of my shift."

"When's that?"

"Ten o'clock."

"MR. GREENE!"

"I'll be there."

ROSIE WAS INDEED THERE when he left the store a few minutes after ten.

"Still gainfully employed?" she asked, her small features trying to look a little cheerful under the hoodie she had popped up over her head.

"Go home, Rosie."

"No."

"Rosie!"

"You are coming with me and we are going to talk this situation out."

"Talking doesn't solve —"

She shut him up by taking him by the hand and pulling him with her down the street. He could feel that her hand was trembling. She held on to him as if she were in a play or a movie, doing what she imagined one was supposed to do when you held hands, but somehow not doing it quite right, keeping them a few feet apart, her arm up at an angle, since he was so much taller than her. It was a very Rosie thing to do, awkward but well-intentioned. Neither of them said anything until they got to the main street. She was heading toward Miranda's neighborhood and wasn't letting go of his hand. It was as if, despite the awkwardness, she finally had him, had finally made her move, and she wasn't going to let this opportunity pass.

As they got nearer Miranda's house, he dropped her hand, almost as if he wanted to turn back.

"Don't worry," she said quietly, "we're not going there. We'll turn up here, a block before her place. I live in Northwood. You can walk me home as we talk. My neighborhood won't impress you, not like where she lives."

"Northwood?"

"That's what they call the little suburb we're in. It's not really a suburb though, not even a separate part of town. It's not old and it's not new, it's not rich and it's not poor. It's like me. Not very noticeable."

"Rosie, you're not —"

"Don't say it, Noah. Don't lie to me, like you lied to Miranda, about anything. We have to talk honestly now."

He didn't say another word until they reached her house, which took them about fifteen minutes. The houses in her area looked like they had been built about thirty years earlier and though all of them weren't exactly alike, it seemed as if each and every one had been designed by the same person and that that person had little imagination. It was as if you could have walked home and mistaken any house here for your own, even though no two were the same.

Rosie stopped when they reached her house. There weren't any cars in the driveway.

"Keeping it all in won't solve anything."

He paused. "Can we go inside?"

"Into my house?" He could see her swallow in the dim light of the street lamp. "Okay ... but only if you talk."

"All right."

"No one's home," said Rosie, still appearing unsure. "We have about half an hour." She held the door open for him, not looking him in the eye. "Welcome to my house." He always wished he could tell Rosie to relax. She had no reason to be so anxious all the time. She was a great girl. Why, he wondered, can't I just tell her that?

He walked inside. She took off her shoes, so he did too. There was a sign above the clothes closet in the vestibule.

Our home is your home. Me Casa, Su Casa.

Rosie noticed him looking at it. She noticed everything.

"I know. Lame. It doesn't get much better once you're inside."

She proceeded to give him a tour of the house. Again, he wished he could tell her just to be herself, but nervousness was simply a part of her. There was no need for a house tour, no need to play host, no need to do anything other than be Rosie. That was more than enough. That would be a good way to put it.

Every room looked like a perfect example of what it was supposed to be, here in this little town at this time in history, and none of it was remarkable. Then they came to her room.

"This ... uh, this is my bedroom." Her face flushed red and he noticed her taking a little breath before they went inside. Everything was ridiculously neat. The walls were white, her covers and pillowcases pink, and there was a Teddy Bear sitting up on the bed, as if it had been placed there to look perfectly at home. There were lots of posters on the walls, all of famous actors and singers, every one of them women. There were two photographs in frames on her desk, and one was of the six of them on the beach. He was between Miranda and her, his shirt off, his arm around Rosie, who was glowing. The other photo was of Miranda, larger than the group shot, smiling warmly at whomever was taking the picture. There were no photos of her parents or siblings.

"This is where I dream," she said, quietly again.

"Hopefully that's true of all of us."

"I mean of being someone." She glanced at the posters. "Let's go downstairs to the rec room. We only have about fifteen minutes now." Rosie was always aware of time.

They padded silently along the thick rug on the hallway, and it seemed as if there was no one in the house, not even them.

"My dad is curling with his buddies. Mom is out with my little sister. She takes her to this ballet school about an hour away. My sister is a lot younger than me. She was a bit of a surprise, but now Mom and Dad can hardly get enough of her."

"Did you take ballet?"

"No. Mom said it was too expensive then."

"Is that it? Just a sister?"

"I have an older brother at university who is doing well. Dad says he thinks he'll be an influential person someday. They're proud of him." She gave a little laugh. "Sit down."

A big, gray u-shaped couch looked toward a large-screen television. He sat down and she sat next to him, her thigh inside her pink jeans almost touching his in his fading black ones. He could actually hear her breathing and even see the slight swell, up and down, of her chest and shoulders.

"This is weird," she said, "just me and you together. No one else around." She shuffled a little farther away.

"Yeah."

She looked up at him. "So, let's talk … about Miranda … about you and her." She kept moving her left hand from her thigh near him to her stomach and back, as if it were a foreign object that she didn't know where to put.

"Why?" he said. "It's all over."

"Don't ... don't say that."

"I was never meant for her. I am not in her league. I have a lot of secrets, Rosie. If you knew about them, you'd know why I'm no match for her. Have you ever noticed that I have never had you guys over to my place? There is a reason for that. My dad —"

"Stop there for a second." She sighed. "Look, Noah, I'm a girl, in case you hadn't noticed, and I'm one of her close friends, which I'm sure you did notice, so she told me all about your situation. Girls, especially girls who are friends, tell each other everything, especially about boys.[42] Sorry to be the bearer of a news flash like that." She looked away at something on the wall. "She told me, and Constance, that you were dishonest with her about some things in the past and she was concerned about that. Though ... she didn't tell me what you said to Lisa Ann when you were alone with her in that change room, when you thought Miranda couldn't hear ... about pretending you'd had sex with her. Maybe it hurt her too much to even say it to us. But I do know it was the final straw. I don't know exactly how you put it ... I hope it wasn't too awful." Her voice had gotten small.

Noah felt his face flush. "Well ... I can't say ..." He looked down. "How bad is all of this? Like, as a girl, how bad would this be to you, if you'd had the sort of relationship we had?"

"It's pretty bad. Horrible, actually."

Panic was flooding through him. "She's gone then, for good."

---

42 Did NOT know this. Pretty terrifying.

Rosie took a deep breath. "Not necessarily."

"What do you mean?"

"Well, you've basically told her that she doesn't matter. You've said that she is just a body to you, that her reputation means nothing to you, that all that you care about is what another girl thinks of you. That's pretty well evil to hear ... even from you ... maybe especially from you."

"Yeah."

"She thought you were different. A different kind of guy. But you were doing little things that concerned her. And then you did a big thing. She thought she had finally found someone, someone for her. She had high expectations, like we all should have in guys, I guess. She thought the two of you were different."

"Yeah."

"So did I."

His eyes began to redden when she said that. He was barely holding on. Rosie noticed, of course, and turned and gave him a quick hug. He could hear her gasp as she held on to him.

"I believe in you, though," she said.

"No one else does." He almost said, *no one who matters does*, but he held that back and hated himself even more for even thinking it. It made him consider that maybe he truly was a piece of shit.

She looked at him.

"I believe in you and Miranda." Now, it seemed like *she* was about to cry.

"Thank you," he said. "That's a nice thing for you to say ...

but it's all over, whether anyone believes in us or not. Miranda doesn't believe in us, that's what matters."

"You have to convince her."

"But I —"

"You have to make her understand that what you said in that change room and the things you've done in the past weren't really you, or at least that they were a part of you that you can fix. You have to convince her that you can do better, be better. She loves you, or at least she did. She wants to think that you are more than what you showed her that day. I think, deep down, she wants to forgive you. She believes in forgiveness; you probably know that. It is going to take a lot of convincing though."

"What if what I said at the beach comes from something inside me that can't be fixed? What if I really am that person who said that horrible thing?"

Rosie gave him a longing look. "I don't believe you are." Slowly, she moved closer to him, her dark eyes locked on his. Her lip was trembling. Then, suddenly, she stood up. "You should go." She turned away and started walking up the stairs.

At the outside door, he put his hand on her shoulder and patted it.

"Thank you, Rosie. Thanks a million. You are … important to me. You are like the sister I never had."

For an instant, Rosie's eyes flared as if in anger, but then she was Rosie again. "If you want to talk more about how you can get her back, I'd be happy to do that. It isn't complicated though. I think you just need to be you, which I guess is actually

both easy and hard. I don't think you should try to impress her.
She's too smart for that. You need to become a person who
would never say what you said. You need to find that person
inside you. I know he's there."

AS NOAH WALKED HOME that night, a strange feeling came
over him. He started worrying about Miranda. He started thinking about how devastated she likely was over all of this. It hit
him that he had not thought of her at all. Maybe it was because
he was sure she was simply mad at him, happy to be through
with him ... but it was more likely because he had only been
thinking of himself. He wondered why he had suddenly realized
this, and then he thought of Rosie, of her looking at him with
longing eyes, of the way she hugged him, held his hand, the
way she had almost kissed him but turned away. He thought of
how she told him she would help him get Miranda back.

By the time he was home, he felt better than he had since
Miranda left him. A bit of the fog was lifting. Could he find a
way to get her back? Could he become a person who deserved
her, could he become a guy, a man, who a girl, a woman,
deserved?

Alone in his little room, he started whispering to himself.

"I am a good person. That is why she liked me in the first
place. I need to understand the ways I'm flawed, though. I need
to try to be better. I need to show her who I really am." He
paused. "I can do it."

He looked at his big wall calendar, the only thing decorating
his room. It covered nine months. He got out the dry erase
marker he used for it. Today was August 31. School started in

seven days. He wrote September on the first month and then each of the next eight months through to the end of May. He put a big star around the word GRAD on June 17, then wrote in large red letters on May 22 — ASK MIRANDA TO THE PROM.

11
Plateau

NOAH KNEW HE HAD a long way to go. He had to re-build himself and he had to make Miranda see it happening. He had nine months. First, though, he had to do perhaps the toughest thing of all: go back to school.

He hadn't seen Miranda for two full weeks when classes began again.

Everyone seemed excited to be back, but no one appeared excited to see him. The crowds parted as he walked down the halls. It seemed as if they wanted to gawk at him or they wanted to sneer. He could handle that, though, and was prepared for it. He had been a bit of an outcast when he first got to the school anyway. His biggest problem would be seeing Miranda.

He didn't have to wait long.

He saw her coming from a distance. She, however, didn't seem to see him. She breezed past him with Constance, who gave him the biggest sneer of all; Bruce, who said, "Hello, Noah Greene"; and Rosie, who glanced at him and then down to the floor. Miranda was laughing and looking amazing, and it did not seem like an act.

"Hey, man, where you been?" asked Walk, running from behind to catch up with Noah. "You go into some sort of witness protection program or something? I must have called you twenty times the last couple of weeks."

Noah didn't respond. He stared straight ahead as he walked, his mouth clenched.

"What sort of a look did Miranda give you?" asked Walk.

"She didn't give me one at all; she acted like I didn't exist, and that's fine."

"Good for you, buddy. Be tough. Forget about her."

"I don't mean that. She's right."

"Huh?"

"I have some growing up to do, and if you think about it, you'll realize that you do too."

"What are you talking about?"

They were at their lockers now and Noah turned on him, eyeballed him. It almost made Walk step back.

"You know what I said about her, right? To Lisa Ann?"

"Uh, yeah, heard it through the grapevine, from Constance. Though I didn't hear exactly —"

"Well, do you think that's right? What I said?"

"Come on, Noah, things happen. Guys are guys and it was Lisa A—"

"Because if you do, then you're an idiot ... and I don't want you around me."

Walk went pale. Noah pulled his old lock out of his back-pack, shoved a few things into his locker, slammed the door shut and locked it.

"I'm asking her out."

"Uh … I don't think that would be a good idea. She's not even in a mood to talk to you, or even look at you. You know Miranda, this could last for a while, like … for a lifetime."

"I'm not doing it now, Walk, you twit. I mean to the prom."

"That's, like, nine months away."

"I'll need all of it. I have an entire person to rebuild. So it's got to start now." He walked away without looking back.

MIRANDA DIDN'T EVEN GLANCE at him in English class, but he didn't care. He had too much work to do, and he knew that any even slightly positive attention he might get from her, he did not deserve … yet. He was determined to do well in this class. Not just well, actually. He wanted to get the best marks, even higher than Miranda's, and this time, this year, he was going to read every word of every book they studied. Last year's class had been Twentieth Century Literature, but this course was the one he and Miranda had been looking forward to all last year and had often talked about: Contemporary Literature. They would be looking at what was out there now, in the twenty-first century. It was an advanced class and only available to students who had high marks last year, so getting the best marks here was going to be quite a task. Some of the works they would study were complex. They would investigate Mantel, Franzen, Zadie Smith, of course, Chimamanda Ngozi

Adichie, Haruki Murakami, Don DeLillo, and Esi Edugyan. All of them awfully heavy. It was like a challenge to the brains of the school. David Foster Wallace would be on the curriculum too, even though most of his work straddled the twentieth and twenty-first centuries. He was a sort of messed-up but brilliant wunderkind of it all.

Noah wondered what it would be like to really read those works, not just start them and cheat. Their first assignment was a Zadie Smith novel called *White Teeth*. They had a week to read it. They were going to do three or four chapters at a time and discuss them as they progressed.

Noah went home after that first class and read the entire book — 480 pages — that night, staying up until five in the morning to finish it. He read every word. Sticking with it through the twelve or thirteen hours it took him to read it produced a surreal experience for him, much more than the episodic, movie-trailer sensation that he had gotten from the other novels he had partially read in the past. He felt as though he was inside the story, sharing souls with the characters, immersed in another world and somehow experiencing deep things in himself too. It was a sort of modern Dickens story,[43] set in contemporary London, full of people of all colors and religions, people with flaws and good sides and puffed-up senses of themselves and their roles on earth, their hatred of themselves, their puniness, and it riveted him. He recognized himself and the world he lived in. When he turned the last

---

43 Miranda would know what I mean.

page, he felt as though he were lifting up toward the ceiling and looking at himself, but not his body, more like his spirit. He had never felt anything like it.

He came back to school the next day exhausted and ready to impress.

"So … the first few chapters of Zadie Smith's *White Teeth*," said Mr. Mitchell. "Any thoughts?"

Noah's hand immediately shot up.

"Mr. Greene?"

"I read the whole thing."

"You didn't need to do —"

"I wanted to. I couldn't put it down." He tried to slide his eyes toward Miranda, but could not completely bring her into frame. From what he could tell, she was staring straight ahead anyway.

He gave another speech, like the one he had offered about *King Lear* … kind of.

"*White Teeth*," he began, "is an extraordinary work of literary art, right from the opening sentence to the final scene. It is an admixture, a potent alloy, of storylines and characters within a multicultural setting, giving one the sense of the great stew of modern life. It is written by a woman who is herself a mixture of origins within a mixed society, a towering talent at the beginning of a remarkable career."

And on and on he went, soon breaking down the novel's style and structure, its subtext, with detailed examples and purple-prosed descriptions, trying way too hard; he could tell from Mr. Mitchell's slightly pained expression when he glanced his way for approval, and a barely audible snicker that came from

somewhere near Miranda. He didn't think it was her, hoped
and prayed it wasn't. He just couldn't stop speaking in this way
though, once he got started.

When he sat down there was silence and he felt embarrassed
and vowed not to do it again. He would have to find more subtle
ways to make it clear that he was reading every book from
cover to cover, and that he continued to be a brilliant interpr-
eter of literary art even at this more challenging level.

That same day, though, right after Contemporary Literature,
he made things worse. As they all headed out into the traffic of
students slouching down the hallways toward their next classes,
he spotted Bruce in the middle of things, standing still, looking
confused, staring down at his schedule. It seemed to Noah that
the papers Bruce held in his hands were actually trembling.
Bruce was used to having all his classes with Miranda, Rosie,
and Constance, but the Contemporary Literature course was
too much for him (he was a science guy, anyway), and Miranda
and Rosie had obviously chosen another course for that period
too. He was all alone. Noah seized upon the opportunity. He
marched toward Bruce.

"Hey, Noh!" cried Walk, definitely not a Contemporary
Literature student either, as he came around a corner and spotted his friend. Walker Jones knew that Noah was not going to
have any admirers this year, had given up those who respected
him when he lost Miranda. He was adamant about staying an
ally. Noah, though, was focused on Bruce and the great chari-
table and loving actions he was about to perform, and that he
knew Miranda was going to see, since she had just come out of
class not far behind Bruce. He didn't even hear Walk.

"Bruce, let me help you!" he said loudly and clearly, his voice rising above the din of conversation. The smaller boy saw him coming toward him and recoiled.

"No!" he shouted. "No, Noah Greene, I intend to do this myself. I must."

As Noah reached him, he glanced back toward Miranda, whom Rosie and Constance were just then intercepting in the hall. Rosie looked toward Bruce and Noah with an expression of horror. She began to shake her head at him.

Noah, however, was on a mission.

"Let me guide you to your next class, my friend," he said loudly, putting his arm around Bruce. He realized that he had never put his arm around him before and wondered why he hadn't.

"NO!" Bruce shouted even louder.

"Just tell me where you have to go."

Noah was getting a little nervous now, his peripheral vision catching Miranda, who had come to a halt; Constance, who was glaring at him; and Rosie, who was still shaking her head and looking upset.

"MIRANDA OWENS TOLD ME I MUST DO THIS ON MY OWN AND I AGREE! I HAVE TO BE INDEPENDENT OR I CANNOT GO ON IN LIFE, NOAH GREENE!" shouted Bruce as Noah reached for the schedule and began to take it from Bruce's quivering grip.

There was silence in the hallway as all the students, it seemed, came to a halt and watched. Lisa Ann Bordeaux was among them, hand-in-hand with the goal-scoring striker on the school's soccer team, whom she had started dating regularly.

"THAT IS WHAT IT IS TO LOVE SOMEONE!" continued Bruce, loudly, "TO TRULY CARE ABOUT THEM, TO THINK OF OTHERS." He ripped the schedule back out of Noah's hand and moved away, heading to his next class.

Miranda walked on, Constance smiled, and Rosie's face looked ashen.

"Sorry," said Noah so quietly that he doubted anyone heard. There was a ripple of laughter. Students started to move again as if they had been re-animated, and he heard several comments about "what an idiot Greene is, what a loser." Even Lisa Ann looked appalled.

It took Walk a little while to come up to his side again.

"Thanks," said Noah quietly.

"For what?"

"Not abandoning me."

"Well," said Walk, "I guess I'm not as bad as I seem."

It appeared to Noah that his friend was a little pissed off when he said this, and it made him think.

LATER THAT DAY, NOAH went to the school's weight room. If he was going to make himself more attractive to Miranda, if he was going to get her to say *yes* when he asked her to the prom in May, he was going to have to make his outside just as attractive as his inside, maybe more so. Girls like strong guys and Miranda couldn't be an exception, though she'd never said much about what she liked in a guy's appearance. She, in fact, had always seemed happy with the way Noah looked.

But he knew that she often worked out in the weight room herself, though it was a wonder that she found the time. When they were a couple, she had tried to coax him to exercise with her, but he had always declined, often using a cute line, he thought, about being a "natural athlete with a God-given manly physique" that didn't need any training. "A slim one, at least," she used to laugh, often grabbing him when she said it. He wondered now if "slim" meant that she thought he was skinny. He needed to bulk up.

Miranda actually stared at him for a second when he entered the room. It was, at best, a look of disbelief.

He headed right for the heavy weights.

First up were dumbbell curls, an exercise that developed the biceps. A bigger set of guns would surely get her attention. The first weight he tried to pick up — not the heaviest dumbbell on the rack but one or two down from that, suitably and impressively massive — almost tore his arm out of its socket when he tried to lift it. Luckily, he didn't drop it on his foot and was able to get it back into the rack using both hands. Hopefully, Miranda hadn't seen that. He cast his gaze down a few notches and picked up another dumbbell. This one was heavy too, heavier than he felt comfortable curling, but there was no way he was going any lower in weight with Miranda possibly watching from the other side of the room. He glanced in her direction. She was turned away, concentrating on an abdominal exercise while balancing on a ball, apparently not the least interested in what he was doing.

He seized another dumbbell and began curling the two heavy weights. His arms were screaming at him, but he made sure he didn't let the slightest groan escape his lips.

He stuck to the exercises that he thought would sculpt his

body in the ways that she would appreciate. He worked on his arms in every which way, on his shoulders, his abs, and his butt. When he left the room, he didn't think he had received even a single glance from Miranda, though she had, maddeningly, spoken to a couple of other guys, both renowned jocks with good bodies. He had never seen her speak to them before.

After marching home in anger, he spent an hour in front of the mirror with his shirt off,[44] examining the progress he hoped he had made and wondering where to go from there.

HE AWOKE THE NEXT morning so sore that he could barely get out of bed. He moved gingerly down the hall at school, doing everything he could not to grimace. Walk noticed.

"What's up?" he asked. "Were you in a car accident or something last night?"

"Just, uh, worked out a little too hard."

"Worked out? You?"

"Shut up, Walk."

"Oh, I get it. You are trying to impress me. Shucks, bro, I like your abs just the way they are, and those biceps and broad shoulders, my, they are —"

"Shut up, Walk."

Miranda didn't even glance at him again when he limped by her a few minutes later. Constance gave him another sneer while Rosie looked like she might giggle as she watched him move as if he were easing across thin ice. He remembered what she said about girls telling each other everything.

---

44 Don't laugh ... again!

He felt like a laughing stock all day and it peaked when he groaned as if he were an old man as he bent over at his desk to pick up a pen he had dropped on the floor. There was a chorus of laughs. It didn't seem to him that Miranda was enjoying any of this, though. She looked straight ahead in class, focused on what she was studying. He vowed to keep going to the weight room to work out, but to take things a little slower next time. He wasn't, however, changing his goals, not a bit.

ON THE WAY OUT of school that day, he discovered something that might help get him back on track. Standing at his locker, pretending to be shuffling through his books, he watched Miranda move past him and head toward the exit. Before she went out, she noticed something on the corkboard where events were posted. Rosie, Constance, and Bruce were with her and they crowded around behind her as she read the information sheet, then pulled out a pen and wrote something down on one of the sticky notes she usually kept at the ready on her binder. Then she handed the pen to the others and they wrote out whatever she had noted too.

Noah was careful to see exactly what she was looking at and then made sure they were all out the door before he sidled over.

HABITAT FOR HUMANITY, read the headline. PLEASE JOIN US TO HELP A FAMILY IN NEED RAISE A HOME. There was a phone number listed for anyone who wanted to volunteer. Noah wrote it down.

"Hey!" cried Walk, stabbing him with a finger in exactly the sorest part of his latissimus dorsi muscles, which he had identified on a chart in the weight room. They form the manly V in the upper back and he figured that Miranda could not help but notice if he could get them perfectly shaped. Right now, though, they were a couple of choice cuts of tenderized meat.

"Ohhh!" he groaned.

"Old man."

"Fart connoisseur."

"What are you doing?"

"Nothing."

Walk glanced at the board. "Habitat for Humanity. Isn't that that thing where a whole bunch of people help build a house for losers?"

"You know you're an idiot, right?"

"Yeah, so why do you keep hanging out with me?"

"Because no one else will and you have potential."

Walk turned a little pale. He lowered his voice. "I say stupid things sometimes, I know. That loser thing ... that was dumb."

"See what I mean? You have potential. Why don't you come out to this thing? I'm going."

"I'm guessing Miranda is too."

"Maybe."

"You've got potential too. Just potential, though."

"I think Constance is coming."

Walk swallowed. "Connie?" he sneered, but it sounded a bit like an act.

WALKER JONES WAS ALREADY up on the roof with a hammer the following week when Noah got to the Habitat for Humanity building site. Constance was right beside him and they were bickering back and forth, though they stuck together the whole day. Miranda was wearing a hard hat and had a carpenter's belt slung around her waist. Noah stopped and stared at her; she was perspiring in her T-shirt and jeans, not even noticing that he was on site. He loved when she looked like this, natural, dressed down — it was simply her without ornamentation. He loved when she looked like anything, actually. The very sight of her literally gave him a pain in his chest. He stood there for a while, his mouth slightly open.

"That's not a good look," said someone next him.

Rosie. She was staring up at him, dressed in the same sort of getup as Miranda, her long, dark brown hair tied in a ponytail, a hand shielding her dark eyes from the sun.

"What?" he said.

"It's not polite to stare."

"Not doing that."

"Right."

"I don't have a hard hat, hammer, nothing."

"There are lots of all of that in the bins." She motioned toward a big black steel container. "There's a list of things you can do on the board above them. Identify one and let the contractor know what you'd like to help out with. She's the one in the white hard hat."

"Thanks."

"Any time."

He started to walk toward the bins.

"Noah?"

"Yeah?"

"Uh, stop trying so hard."

He couldn't stop, though. Miranda was right there, looking

like a gift from God,[45] and he had to impress her. He only had eight months left now. He gave the list of chores a quick run-through and found the one that seemed to him to be the most spectacular, high on the roof — even higher than Constance and Walker, who were nailing studs at the peak. He looked skyward. There was only one guy up there now and he was an adult, big and powerful looking, at home in the heavens, likely a roofer or something.

When he volunteered, the contractor gave him a quick once-over.

"Are you athletic?"

"I, uh, play on the basketball team at school."

"Okay. Anything else?"

"I, uh, lift weights, work out regularly."

"Would your parents be good with this?"

"Sure."

"Well, I'm going to ask that you tie yourself to the safety ropes up there. Don't want you to fall. Even Bud uses them." She glanced toward the roofer at the peak. "Be careful on your way up and ask him to help you fasten yourself on."

It went well for the first hour. Then Noah started to tire and got careless. He had been glancing down regularly to see if Miranda was watching, but he had never once seen her so much as glance up. Rosie, on the other hand, looked toward him every now and then, her hand shielding the sun from her eyes again, her posture tense, as if concerned for his safety.

"Eyes on the job," said Bud. "Won't impress whoever you're

---

45 Well ... it's the way I feel, no exaggeration.

trying to be a hero to if you fall." Bud smelled of the smokes twisted into the shoulder of his dirty T-shirt, had slicked-back white hair, a craggy face, and was a bit thick around the middle, but he moved around the roof like some sort of pot-bellied simian.

I'm not falling, thought Noah, *not ever, not ever again in any way.* "Take a chance," he whispered to himself. "She'll never notice if you don't do something that stands out." He paused for a second, his hands shaking a little, the sweat soaking the Bob Dylan T-shirt Miranda had bought him. "Let's see what she thinks of this." He stood up on a stud.

"Whoa," said Bud.

Down below, people were looking up, quite a few people. The boy at the peak of the roof was standing there like a weather vane, like an ornament in the sky.

It seemed to Noah that he lost his balance in slow motion and started to fall slowly too. It appeared to take forever. *I'm falling*, he said inside his head. *I'm falling and she won't like this. I am a failure. I am about to die.*

As he dropped below the frame of studs and headed toward the hard ground thirty feet below, Bud reached for him. His thick hand and meaty fingers could not hold on, though, and Noah fell from his grasp.

The ropes, however, did their job, leaving him hanging like a clown a yard or two below the frame at the peak, swinging gently back and forth, as a searing pain shot through his groin. There was silence for a moment and then laughter from below, a great deal of it.

Bud, whose latissimus dorsi were indeed well-developed, as

was every other muscle in his body, had no problem pulling him up.

"Error," he said to Noah, who was pale. "Sit here for a little while and relax, kid." After a few minutes, Bud went on, talking as he hammered. "You know, my man, us guys are idiots. It takes us a long time to mature. The ladies have that over us. They are older than us from the moment they come out of the womb. It's taken me a long time to realize that I need to think before I act. Acting, being active and physical, that's a bit of a strength for us guys and that's not a bad thing ... but you have to think too."

THAT NIGHT, NOAH FELT like he had indeed been in a car accident. But as he lay in bed, it was his emotional wounds he was licking. He tried to ignore his father's moan in the next room; he needed to come up with a more effective game plan. He decided on two things, things he figured had to impress Miranda: one intellectual and the other physical.

The first involved a lot more reading.

"I need to do more than just read the books in the Contemporary Literature course," he told himself. "I need to take it to another level. I need to read just about everything she might admire. I need to be able to talk about books super intelligently to her." He wracked his brain to remember the books she had mentioned she thought were great, and important in the history of literature. He thought of Dante's *Divine Comedy*, of a book called *Ulysses* by James Joyce, *Invisible Man* by Ralph Ellison, a few by Doris Lessing, a series by Elena Ferrante, and others by Vladimir Nabokov. Then he thought of the big one, that difficult and long novel by David Foster Wallace called *Infinite Jest*. He remembered that night at the Owens' house where he had pretended to be reading Wallace. He recalled what Miranda had said about *Infinite Jest*. It was more than a thousand pages long, "including footnotes." Footnotes? Really? That truly was weird for a novel. "You should try to read all of it," she had said, "if you can, because it's worthwhile. I think you are up to it." That sounded like a challenge he needed to take on. He knew that some guys pretended to have read it to impress smart girls.

That made Noah stop. "Is that what I'm doing?" he asked himself. "Is that sort of thing a terrible fact about boys, period?"

Samantha Owens hadn't liked David Foster Wallace as a human being and Miranda had said he had been a "jerk" at times, but that maybe Wallace knew it, maybe knew guys were jerks a lot of the time and that some of his writing, especially his later work, seemed to indicate that he wanted to be better.

Noah got up and went to his laptop to check out more about the writer. On his way, he passed by the little book by Wallace called *This Is Water*, sitting on his bedside table, the one that Miranda had given him that night, handing it to him like it was something precious. He thought of her repeating those three words at times during the days when they were happy and together. She had said it as a mantra, as if it were something that was important to remember. He kept the book on the bedside table because it was a prize to him, a sign of his worth, like a medal or something. He had never thought of it as a book and hadn't bothered to read it all the way through. It seemed so small and insubstantial. He considered reading it now. No, he told himself, he'd do that later. He had his thoughts set on *Infinite Jest*.

The information about Wallace's life indicated that he indeed wasn't perfect, though in some ways he seemed like a cool guy too, kind of looked like Axl Rose, the lead singer dude in Guns N' Roses, and everybody said he was a genius with a brain filled with knowledge that moved at a million miles an hour. Zadie Smith even said it.[46] That extraordinary mind allowed him to write some of the greatest works of the last hundred years. He was seen as a sort of poster boy of modern angst too. He was apparently an amazing teacher, a professor who was idolized and loved by his students. He suffered from serious depression and anxiety, wrote about it often, and in the end those devils had done him in, causing him to take his own life in a shocking act that broke the hearts of his many admirers. His work, apparently, was not only brilliant, but extremely funny, and conveyed truths about modern life and life period. He wrote stellar short stories, riveting non-fiction, and a few novels, including *Infinite Jest*, a work looked upon as one of the best novels of the modern era. Apparently, he once said that "Art that is alive and urgent is art that is about what it is to be a human being. I write stuff about what it feels like to live, instead of being a relief from what it feels like to live."[47] Noah loved that.

Wallace had slept with some of his college students and had sometimes been callous in things he said to women. He

46 I found a quote where she said he had "no equal among living writers. He was an actual genius."

47 I found these quotes in interviews with him on YouTube.

had a relationship with another writer, an accomplished non-fiction author named Mary Karr, during which she said he had been abusive to her, stalking her and shoving her hard at least once.[48] This was before he got married to someone who he appeared to have treated kindly. His death had devastated his wife. It was also before he wrote *This Is Water*. It was popular, it seemed. In fact, there appeared to be more about it online than anything else to do with Wallace. There were some critical comments about it as well, though: that it was too popular, just "pabulum for the masses," "trite," and beneath the rest of his work.

Noah glanced over at *This Is Water* again. "Better to start with his other stuff," he said to himself. He also immediately started to ponder the problem of how to make Miranda aware that he was reading *Infinite Jest*. As that thought began to form, a voice inside told him he was being shallow. He ignored it though. He could not afford to listen to it.

OVER THE NEXT FEW months, Noah threw himself at an enormous workload, intellectual and physical. He kept going to the weight room, he spent twice as much time on schoolwork as he used to, he made sure he improved at every basketball practice and in every game, and he read and read and read. He seemed to be checking out a book a day from the library.

The Divine Comedy was boring but worthwhile. Doris Lessing's *The Golden Notebook* was about the same. Nabokov's *Lolita* was flat-out weird. Ellison's *Invisible Man* a revelation.

---

48 It didn't seem like these accusations were made public until after his death, so he actually never responded to them.

And James Joyce's *Ulysses* was only readable when Noah found other books that explained it almost line by line. Then, it seemed incredible. It made him gulp to think how brilliant Miranda was. He tried reading more women authors too, realizing that he hadn't experienced as many as he should. He read Joyce Carol Oates, Isabel Allende, Eleanor Catton, Jennifer Egan, Paula Fox, and several more. When it came to Wallace, Noah started with a collection of his non-fiction, something called *Consider the Lobster*, and found it smart and funny; the stories seemed to remove the bullshit from life and tell the truth. Most of it made you feel like you were having a conversation with some brilliant guy who knew what was really going on. His short stories were awesome too: a strange mixture of witty and incredibly sad, frighteningly so sometimes, and sometimes bizarre. They made you think, almost hurt your brain when you let yourself contemplate them deeply. There were lots of amazing characters and imaginative plots and screwed-up people ... mostly screwed-up guys. A collection called *Brief Interviews with Hideous Men*, when he understood it, made Noah feel embarrassed to be a member of the male gender. He wondered if Wallace was a "hideous man" himself, like Noah Greene, telling terrible truths.

Then, he took a crack at *Infinite Jest*.

Whoa.

He read the first few pages and couldn't figure out exactly what was going on. It seemed to be about a guy who was applying for entrance into a college and was freaked out about it, freaked out period, sitting there in a room full of adults who were judging him. That connected with Noah.

Parts of the book gave him a funny feeling — they made him think about what it was like to be extremely nervous, anxious in a way that he had remembered sometimes being, or almost being. At those moments in his life, he had felt very alone. Reading those parts scared him. The whole opening section was hard work to get through and when he reached the point where he felt a bit lost, when the scene changed to something completely different that didn't seem connected at all, he had to stop. The chapters didn't have numbers, but had strange titles like "Year of the Depend Adult Undergarment" and "Year of Glad." He told himself he would try again. He *must* try again.

The next day he took his copy of *Infinite Jest* with him to school. It was thick, its cover a prominent sky-blue with a wisp of a cloud on it and the title in big yellow letters. It quickly occurred to Noah that he could carry the book in such a way that anyone coming anywhere near him would be able to read the title. He spent a good deal of time that morning in front of his mirror at home positioning the book so it was as visible as possible.[49] Unfortunately, when he passed Miranda in the hallway, she was usually on his right side and he always carried his books in his left hand. He tossed them over to his right and examined that look in the mirror. It felt and appeared awkward. He would have to get used to it.

HE HAD BARELY GOTTEN through the school's front doors when Walker approached and started things off in a decidedly bad way.

---

49 Not proud of this, but again, in novels you have to tell the truth.

"What the hell is that?" he asked. "No, let me guess: Shakespeare's entire collection with as many boring essays about it as can be found."

"It's a novel."

"You've got to be kidding me. It looks more like an anvil. Do you want me to help you carry it?"

Other kids were starting to pass them. A few glanced down at the big book. It seemed to him as if a couple of girls' eyes widened when they saw it. None of that mattered, though. He was looking for Miranda.

"If you're going to say anything about it," said Noah quietly, "at least say something nice."

"About that?" said Walk, pointing at the book. "Hey ... it IS Shakespeare! That's one of the famous things he said, isn't it? 'Infinite jest'?"

"Not bad, Walk. I guess you must have listened a little in class."

"Yeah, I remember it because it was in a graveyard scene, wasn't it? Didn't one of the characters pick up a skull or something, like, a real skull, and talk about some guy who used to be, like, the skull?"

"Yeah, in *Hamlet*. It's about how tragic life is, how ridiculous we all are, really. How we roll along and don't think a lot about life, and laugh about things, and maybe think our lives are important ... but we all die. We end up a skull ... we end up like this useless *'fellow of infinite jest'*."

"Nice."

"But this isn't Shakespeare."

"Probably just as boring, though."

"Come on, Walk, say something nice about it, good and loud."

"Eh?" They took another couple of strides, Walker noticing how Noah was regarding everyone who passed as if they were his audience. "You're acting weird, Noh. You're walking weird too ... don't you usually carry your books on the other side?"

As he said that, Miranda came around the corner past the chemistry lab. Same crew — Rosie, Bruce, and Constance.

"Oh," said Walker. "Con ... I mean, Miranda and her gang."

Noah shifted the book in his hand to make the title more visible and it slipped from his grasp and dropped to the floor, smashing onto Walker's toes inside his thin running shoes.

"Ow!"

It occurred to Noah that this was actually a good thing. Walk's shout had grabbed everyone's attention, and the book had flipped over and landed almost right at Miranda's feet. She couldn't miss it.

"Sorry," said Noah and reached down to pick it off the floor. As he did, he glanced up and noticed that Miranda was staring at the cover of the book. Then, she stared at him. Their eyes hadn't met since the moment she left him. His heart pounded. He looked into those beautiful, pale blue eyes and just about swooned. *Oh my God*, he thought. But almost as quickly as she glanced at the book and at him, she looked away.

"Crap, Noah, that hurt!" said Walk.

"*Infinite Jest*," said Rosie, looking down at it and then at him. He could see her swallow. "That looks long. Is it a good book ... Noah?"

He felt horrible. He could sense that Rosie Gonzalez knew

what was going on, the game he was playing. She had decided to play along too. She was willing to help him, even though he could tell by the color in her face and her guilty expression that she knew he was doing this simply to put a move on Miranda — a deceitful and dishonest one.

"Yes," said Noah quietly. "I'm reading it."

"Well, why else would you be carrying it around?" said Constance. It was the first thing she'd had said to him in months.

"That's impressive," said Rosie. "... That you're reading it." She looked down at her feet.

NOAH HID THE BOOK from view for the rest of the day. When he went home, he tried to read more and got a little further, though still not always understanding what was going on. Eventually he didn't care — the writing was so amazing. He started reading it out loud — not so loud that his father could hear, but loud enough that he could feel the rhythm of the sentences and the interplay of the words, and the way in which the characters' manners of expressing themselves made them so real. Part of the plot, such as there was one, swirled around presenting a bunch of different scenes about this brilliant, mentally messed-up, young guy who was introduced in the first scene. The character's name was Hal Incandenza — Noah wondered if the name might be a play on Hamlet. Hal was a good tennis player and smart too, but he came from a messed-up family. There were scenes at the tennis academy school he went to — that his physically and mentally challenged brother attended too — where his bizarre mother reigned and had an ongoing affair with a young student named John Wayne, and where his father, an artsy filmmaker who had committed suicide by somehow putting his head into a microwave, had once ruled. His father had made a movie called *Infinite Jest* that caused people who saw it to keep watching and do nothing else. It was sort of lethal. There were scenes in a drug and alcohol addiction clinic down a hill from the tennis academy, some Quebec terrorists in wheelchairs, and a couple of unusual secret agents who were at least triple agents, maybe more, one of them a cross-dresser. There were indeed tons of footnotes[50] and Noah found it weird to be reading a novel and flipping back and forth to read passages full of information at the back of the book. Even when Noah wasn't getting what was going on, he understood — or maybe the better word was "felt" — that this multilayered story was telling him something about our messed-up modern world and our messed-up selves trying to survive in it, all of us like actors — self-conscious ones. It was a world full of entertainment, drugs, depression, and environmental disaster, and was led by the United States as it sucked up and dominated its entire continent, America — a world that lacked people who cared enough about others. He found himself both fascinated and embarrassed to be a human being. When he had had enough for the night, his mind buzzed. He was amazed at how much of it he had read. He put the book away in his bedside table and vowed to keep it there, out of sight, when he was not reading it.

That seemed to him to be a step forward.

---

50 Endnotes, to be more precise.

12

Turning Point

THE NEXT DAY, HE he took a step back again. He couldn't help himself.

It started when Miranda came to his basketball game. As Noah was sitting on the bench for a brief rest, he was shocked to see her enter the gym.

Noah had been a bench player last year, but his workouts and his drive to be better at everything had pushed him into the starting lineup, his value based on how hard he worked, as well as his commitment to playing responsibly both defensively and offensively.

He stood up, though, when he saw Miranda and looked toward Coach Beatty, letting him know he wanted back in. It was a good two minutes before he was supposed to go back into the game. The coach stressed a team approach where everyone got to play at least a few minutes. The teammate who had replaced him had only been on the court for a short while. But Beatty relented.

"All right," the coach said. "You must be ready to roll. Get in there, Greene!"

Noah ran onto the court a little faster than he normally did. He was a point guard, the player who controlled play, who distributed the ball. He could see the game well, was a good passer, and though he could score too, he often gave up opportunities in order help the team win and get the ball to teammates who were perhaps a little more skilled offensively.

Not today though.

When he brought the ball up the court this time, right toward the end of the gym where Miranda was sitting, he had his eye on doing something spectacular. As he came within a few strides of the top of the key, he faked a pass to the best three-point shooter on the team, who had shaken the opponent covering him and was open for a shot in a spot from where he rarely missed. Noah, however, did not intend to get the ball to him, not with Miranda close by, likely riveted on the action. He sped up, snapped the ball behind his back and around to his left hand, elevated above the two defenders now keyed on him, drifted to the left of the basket while in the air, and deftly kissed the ball off the glass and into the hoop.

There was a whoop of delight from the crowd, but no reaction other than disbelief from his coach, his teammates, and especially the team's best shooter, standing there for a good five seconds in the spot where he would have made three points, instead of Noah's crowd-pleasing two.

Noah glanced toward Miranda, but she seemed to be just sitting there, not even applauding, her attention more on the guy who should have taken the shot than on him.

"Use your teammates!" shouted Coach Beatty. He didn't sound too displeased though. He knew Noah was a team player and, in fact, he had often pushed him to be a little more selfish on the court and not give up so many of his own opportunities.

But Noah kept doing it, ignoring the situation. It was halfway through the fourth quarter, the score was close, the opponent was a big rival, and the game a key one — its outcome would decide whether or not the team would qualify for the regional tournament. Coach Beatty assumed Noah had that uppermost in mind, but he did not know the full powers of Miranda Owens.

Noah kept ignoring opportunities to pass, trying instead to score almost every time he came down the court, and usually in the most eye-catching way he could — behind-the-back dribbles, long-range jumpers, hook shots, even one attempt to dunk. Soon, the other team figured out that he wasn't passing and double-teamed and even triple-teamed him. Though he scored a few times at first, it didn't take long before they were stopping him every time up the court and his teammates, out of position because they couldn't figure out what he was going to do, were often stranded in the offensive end of the court, unable to get back on time to be effective defensively. Slowly, the other team took charge of the game, Noah's teammates stopped giving him the ball … and Coach Beatty took him out of the game, glowering at him when he sat him down, the contest now out of reach.

Noah slumped onto the bench, heaving, looking across the court toward Miranda. She wasn't looking back. Again, her attention seemed to be on someone else.

When the game ended, his teammates wouldn't talk to him. That, however, didn't concern him. He had never been a fan of being popular among the other boys anyway. But something else did bother him.

Miranda.

She had actually walked across the court to speak to another player: Andrew Chen. The guy with the great three-point-shooting ability; the guy Noah had refused to give the ball to, probably costing them the game.

What pissed off Noah was that Miranda seemed interested in talking to this guy and even put her hand on his shoulder once, almost in consolation. What upset him the most, though, was that Andrew Chen, tall and handsome, was a nice guy.

He could barely describe how he felt as he stood there watching them. It was as if to her, and maybe to everyone else, he had never existed.

HE WALKED HOME THAT night feeling desperate.

Then he turned away from his normal route and headed toward Constance Mark's house. He wasn't even going to text her before he showed up.

He knew where she lived. Walk had told him: in a nice old house not far from Miranda's. It was almost time for dinner when he got there and there was no answer at first when he rang the doorbell. Inside, he heard distant voices, then a bit of an argument about who should answer the door and finally a boy, about ten or eleven, violently opened it.

The two males stared at each other for a few seconds. The kid was dressed in clothes that looked too fashionable and grown-up for him: an expensive-looking black hoodie, cool designer running shoes, and red pants.

"Yeah?" he said, sounding bored and distracted. He had a video game controller in his hands and appeared impatient. He didn't wait for Noah to answer.

"CONSTANCE!" he shouted. "IT'S FOR YOU. ONE OF YOUR DUMB FRIENDS! A GUY!" He smirked at Noah. "Don't mean anything by that man, just, you know, talking to my sister. Come on in. Gotta go." He darted away down the hall and turned into what appeared to be the living room or a family room. Noah could see the reflection of the animation in a video game moving across a window, apparently coming from what appeared to be a rather large flat-screen television.

"A guy?" shouted Constance from somewhere deeper in the house, farther down the hallway, possibly the kitchen. There was a pause. "Who?" Then another pause. "Mario? Who?"

Then she appeared. She was wearing the sort of thing she usually wore — black leggings with a top that hung down almost to her knees — though this time she actually had an apron on. Her black hair was a bit disheveled and looked wilder than usual, getting in her eyes. She stopped in her tracks the moment she saw Noah.

"Oh," she said.

It was the nicest thing she had ever said to him.

When she started to talk again, she almost seemed nervous.

"What brings you here?" she asked. She sounded sort of sarcastic, but she looked flustered.

"Just, uh ... just came by to talk."

"Really?" The minute that word came out of her mouth, it looked like she regretted it. "Probably about Miranda. Look, I'm not helping —"

"No, not about Miranda. It is over between us."

"Then, about what?" Constance seemed suddenly to notice her apron and quickly took it off. "I don't have much time. I'm making dinner. That always falls to me."

"Yeah, I noticed. Sorry. I guess your mom and dad aren't —"

"I don't have a dad. He kind of died. Mom is out, still working. She's at the safe house. You know, the one on Intersection?"

"No."

"Figures. There are lots of women, even in this town, who need help, you know, from men who mean them harm."

"That's awful, but she is doing something that is definitely worthwhile then."

Constance looked at him and was silent. She narrowed her eyes.

"I'm sorry about your dad. I didn't know," he added.

"Yeah, well, how could you? You never asked. He got sick and died when Mom was pregnant with Mario. It all happened fast. Mario is the man of the house now. You can see how useful he is."

"Can we just talk?"

"About what?'

"Anything. I feel badly about how we never talked. I guess I was blinded by Miranda."

Constance was silent again.

"I'll help you make dinner."

"What do you want, Noah?"

"Nothing. Really. Absolutely nothing. I just want to talk."

It took a while before she turned and motioned for him to follow her into the kitchen.

"Con-stance has a boy-friend!" sang Mario as he watched them pass from his seat on the sofa in the family room. "Better than that other dude," he called out. "That Walker guy."

"Walk has been here?" asked Noah as they entered the kitchen — a renovated one with a marble island, butcher block countertops, and stainless-steel appliances.

"Yeah," was all she said, without even turning to look at him.

"What did he want?"

She went back to cutting carrots, wielding a knife that seemed far too big for the job and driving it down hard onto the wooden counter with each chop. "Do you want to talk or not?"

"Yeah, sure."

"Then, talk."

And so they did. Not for just a little while, either. Noah kept the conversation going for almost an hour, making sure that he said almost nothing about himself. Constance was reluctant to say much at first, often checking her phone on the counter, responding with terse answers and waiting for the next question, but eventually she opened up. He quickly discovered that the way to get her to elaborate was to ask about her father. At times she seemed almost angry at him for dying, but at other moments would forget herself and talk about how caring he was and how much he did for people, working as a pro bono lawyer for the poor in town. Once that subject appeared to be exhausted, Noah started apologizing, or at least appearing to be expressing regrets. He said he was sorry for about a million things: from the way he had seldom talked to her, to what he worried were his sometimes dismissive ways about her feminist views, his "boy-attitudes," and finally to what he had said to Lisa Ann about Miranda. By the time he got to that last subject, Constance seemed to soften. She didn't say anything, though, about the Miranda comment. A few moments later, she got a text on her phone.

"My mother says she'll be home in a few minutes," said Constance.

"I'd better get going."

"You ... you don't have to."

"No, I'd better be on my way home."

"I, uh, know about the way things are for you."

"So I hear; the girls' grapevine, right?"

Constance actually smiled. "Yeah. Sorry it's like that for you," she added in a small voice.

When they were at the door, he opened it to go and then turned back to her.

"If you, uh, see Miranda, maybe you could let her know that I stopped by."[51]

Constance's face went red. "And that you were so kind and caring? That you asked me all about myself? That you are such a wonderful —"

---

51 Yeah, I actually said that.

"I didn't mean —"

"Get out, you jerk!"

She shoved him through the door and slammed it.

He stood on the doorstep for a moment, hating himself. He remembered something he'd read in *This Is Water* when he was flipping through it, reading bits, trying to find things that he could remember to quote back to Miranda. One part had stood out because she had once referred to it: it said that all human beings are selfish, that our default position is selfish, that we are always the center of the world to ourselves, that we see everything through our own needs and interests. He had a feeling that the rest of the little book was about trying not to be that way. *This Is Water*. Miranda's mantra. He thought again of what he had said to Lisa Ann.

He truly did hate himself.

He started walking down the street, and Constance's mother passed by in her car and pulled into her driveway. He turned and watched her get out of the little vehicle, her cell phone pinned between her chin and shoulder, likely talking to someone about how she could help them, someone desperately in need.

He walked a few blocks with his mind a blank.

"Noah?"

It seemed to him that Rosie had appeared out of thin air. She was walking along the sidewalk on the other side of the street. She crossed over to him.

"You don't look good," she said.

"Thanks."

"What are you doing around here?" She glanced up the street past Constance's house toward Miranda's.

"No," he said, "I wasn't there. I'm not stalking her."

Rosie didn't look convinced. "Do you know someone else on this street?"

"Yeah, Constance."

"Constance?"

"I, uh, went to her house to talk with her."

"Why?"

They were standing about three or four feet from each other, Rosie looking up at him with her arms crossed in front of her chest.

"So ... so I could appear to be a nice person."

"I don't follow you."

"I went there, Rosie, to have a deep conversation with Constance, a kind and caring conversation that was not about me or my needs or my breakup ... so that Constance would tell —"

"Miranda," said Rosie sternly. She seemed to tighten her grip on herself.

"Yeah."

There was silence for a moment.

"Well," she finally said, "I guess that about sums you up." She looked like she was about to cry. "Goodbye, Noah," she added and walked away from him without turning back.

NOAH TRUDGED HOME FEELING numb. He was beyond hating himself now. He had been exposed for what he really was to even Rosie, the one person he thought would never give up on him.

He could hear his father snoring when he was still out in

the hallway. When he got into his room, two objects seem to glow at him: big *Infinite Jest* and little *This Is Water*. He picked up the first one and threw himself onto his bed, starting in where he had left off last time. It was slow-going again. The story shifted back and forth between narratives, delving into different stories and different times. The chapters were not long — it was like rapid fire. He still couldn't figure out why the chapters were titled the way they were: *The Year of the Tuck's Medicated Pad* and *The Year of the Trial-Size Dove Bar*, etc. He couldn't figure out what era the novel was set in, either. It seemed sort of contemporary but sometime in the near future too. An entertainer was the president of the United States,[52] or at least the leader of a drug-addled, sport-and-TV-fixated, wall-to-wall entertainment, environmentally destructive, secret-intelligence-infested monster country that seemed to have gobbled up all of "America," adding Canada and Mexico. Even though Noah didn't get exactly what was happening, he continued to connect with the characters, especially the smart but messed-up young Hal. The writing was whip-crack smart, snapping and crackling on the page like fireworks. It went on and on though, and after a while, he gave up. He wasn't about to ever speak to Miranda about this novel anyway. He looked over at the little white book, *This Is Water*, again. He picked it up and started to read.

Twenty minutes later he was done. It was so different from anything else he had read by Wallace, his earlier stuff, at least on the surface. It was so unadorned and honest. Part of him

---

52 This was long before Donald Trump was president, two decades before, in fact.

thought that what it was saying was dumb and obvious, but another part knew that it was right — about life and about him.

He got down on his knees on the floor and leaned against his bed. He started to cry. Then, he began to pray. He asked for forgiveness, and he asked for the strength to be a good person.

By the time he had his clothes off and was in bed with the covers up, he felt better than he had felt for a long time. He also had an idea.

When he asked Miranda to the prom on May 22, he was going to give her a present. He knew what it would be. He would write a novel — a short one — for her. It would be about what happened to them, how he might have changed after she left him (he would see about that), and how it all turned out, right up until he asked her to the prom. The climax would be her answer. It was going to be real-life, some of it occurring as he wrote it. He didn't know what would happen at the end. He knew the title, though: "The Book of Us."[53] He also knew the quotation he would use at the beginning of the book:

Everyone worships. The only choice we get is what to worship.

---

53 Some of the other possibilities? "I Want You," "Water," "Novel Idea," "You and Me," "This is Us," "Us," (found out both those last two are taken, rats) "The Gift," "My Choice" "The Book of You and Me."

13
Two New Friends

THE NEXT DAY, AFTER coming home and making his father an early supper, Noah went to Bruce King's house. He arrived at about 5:30. Thank goodness Miranda had insisted on them walking Bruce home the night of the Hitchcock movie or Noah would not have had a clue where Bruce lived. It wasn't the sort of thing he had ever taken any interest in. He realized he had never talked to Bruce in any depth about anything, really. He had simply categorized him as this messed-up kid and taken the default position of worrying about what mattered to Noah Greene, not to Bruce, Constance, or Rosie … or, he realized now, even Miranda.

He didn't want to text ahead of time this time either; he just wanted to show up.

The Kings' house was on the wealthiest street in town, right in the central area on a wide avenue that dissected the main street and led up to an old college, a magnificent white stone building now used as a home for senior citizens. The street was lined with three-story mansions with huge lawns, each house more than a hundred years old. When Noah got up onto the veranda of Bruce's home, he felt like an intruder, and not because he didn't fit in this neighborhood; his footsteps made the stained wooden floor creak. He had to talk himself into ringing the doorbell. As he stood there trying to work up the courage to do so, he noticed that the entire street seemed unusually quiet and that absolute silence appeared to reign inside the King home.

He rang the bell.

Silence prevailed again at first. Then, he heard light footsteps approaching and a young woman opened the inside door and looked through the glass at him.

"May I help you?" she asked. She was small and earnest looking.

"I ... I'm Bruce's friend. Come for a visit?"

"What is your name?"

"Noah. Noah Greene."

"Just a moment."

She walked away. A minute later, she returned and opened the door.

"My name is Angelica, the Kings' employee. I live here too. Bruce will see you. Go upstairs, turn left, and go all the way down to the end of the hallway. I told him to leave the door open."

"Thank you." The place was sparkling; the hardwood floors gleamed, the banister and newel posts on the old staircase were

THE BOOK OF US

polished to perfection, and even the black-and-white photographs on the walls shone. Noah took a step but noticed Angelica glaring down at his shoes. He took them off and slipped up the stairs.

Bruce was seated in a leather chair in his bedroom, focused on his laptop and his phone as Noah entered. He swiveled around and his face went from bleary-eyed to glowing as he took in his visitor.

"NOAH! NOAH!"

"Just one of me, Bruce."

"Very funny, Noah Greene!"

Noah glanced around the room. The curtains were pulled closed and almost every inch of the walls and much of the ceiling were papered with posters: great stretches of *Black Panther*, *Star Wars*, and *Lord of the Rings* scenes and characters. Wakanda, Alderaan, and Hobbiton glowed like paradises. T'Challa, Bilbo Baggins, Han Solo, and even creepy Gollum stared at Bruce and anyone else who entered. It made the room seem crowded. Bruce was never alone.

"What brings you here at 5:36 p.m. on a Thursday evening in mid-December?"

"Just wanted to hang out."

"With me?"

"No, with Harrison Ford."

"Well, then, Noah Greene, you have erred. Mr. Ford, of *Star Wars* and Indiana Jones and Jack Ryan fame, lives in Los Angeles, California, the City of Angels, and in Jackson, Wyoming, a popular holiday resort area for rich Americans. Both these locations are in the country Americans, and some citizens of other countries, I am afraid, like to call America, but it is really not, just the United States of America, with his wife, Miss Calista —"

"That was a joke."

"I am aware of that," said Bruce, grinning at him. Then he arrested his smile. "I know why you are here." His face grew grim.

"Miranda?"

"Yes."

"Well, then you would be wrong, Bruce King of incredible knowledge of nerdy things fame."

"I would?"

"Absolutely. In fact, if you so much as breathe a word to Miss Owens about my visit here today, I will roll up one of your *Star Wars* posters and beat you with it."

"You will?" Bruce swallowed.

"No, but don't tell her. Okay?"

Bruce smiled. "Okay."

They spent the next hour together, mostly talking, Noah trying to get a word in edgewise as Bruce, unleashed and with permission to talk, regaled him with facts about more things than he ever wanted to know.[54] Noah tried to keep up, though. He tried to empathize with Bruce's need to say these things and found himself basking in the glow of knowing that he was making this unusual kid feel happy. Bruce's face was nearly

---

54 Subjects ranged from the color of John and Hank Green's eyes to how to tie a Windsor knot, backwards, to Neil deGrasse Tyson's degrees and where he earned them, to the population of Saskatoon, Saskatchewan in every census from 1901 until the present. I'll mention a few more later, in Bruce's words, to do it all justice.

split with a smile throughout their conversation. He leaned forward in his chair and spoke at high speed, his conversation in need of footnotes, many of his sentences beginning with, "Did you know ..."

When Angelica called Bruce for dinner, he looked disappointed.

"Angelica, who knows nothing about the Kingdom of Wakanda or a galaxy far, far away, but is in possession of interesting facts about the cost of all of her fifty pairs of shoes and her salary relative to dozens of people employed in similar jobs to hers, is calling me and I must go. She has looked after me for many years. She is a nice lady."

"Yes, I met her. Where are your mother and father?"

"Mother, Gwyneth King, is a lawyer, large law firm in the city, and father, David King, does the same. They commute. Should be home soon, actually." He looked at his watch. "Estimated time of arrival, ETA, usually about 6:41 pm, Eastern Standard Time."

They walked down the stairs together. When they were halfway there, two people entered the front door, talking, one on her phone and speaking to the person behind her at the same time. When they saw Bruce and Noah on the stairs, they stopped in their tracks. David King closed the door behind them.

"I'll call you back," said Mrs. King into her phone.

"Angelica?" said Mr. King loudly.

Their employee was immediately in the hallway, the aroma of a lovely meal trailing behind her.

"Who is this?" asked Mrs. King, pointing up the stairs, but speaking to Angelica.

"It's a —" began Angelica.

"I'm Noah Greene," said Noah.

"A friend of mine!" cried Bruce.

"A friend?" said Mr. King.

"Yes! Noah Greene, recipient of the second-best marks in all literature courses at our school, behind ..." His voice trailed off.

"Have you been here long?" asked Mrs. King.

"Uh," said Noah, "for an hour or so, I guess."

"What have you two been doing?" asked Mrs. King.

"Conversing on a myriad of subjects, Mother! Though I will leave out some things, I can attest, off the top of my head, that we spoke of some interesting plot twists in the fourth *Star Wars* movie, things that affect the whole hero myth in interesting ways, and then our discussion ranged to distant subjects. In fact, when Angelica called us, we were getting to the assassination of Mr. John Fitzgerald Kennedy, former president of the United States of America and womanizer and why —"

"We don't need to know all that, Bruce, too much information," said his father. "I've told you that many times."

"Are you all right?" asked his mother. "You look tired."

"I am fine. I took my pulse several times."

"No need for that either."

"And it was normal. I am guessing my body temperature is at or near 98.6 degrees as we speak."

"Glad to hear it." David King reached out for Noah's hand. "A pleasure to meet you, Mr. Greene. Have we met before? Bruce has just a few friends. Only three girls ever drop by, and a boy, once, recently."

"Master Walker Jones, somewhat shy and reactive, but with real potential," said Bruce.

"Really? He was here?" asked Noah.

"Twice."

"It seems you were just leaving?" asked Mrs. King.

"Yes."

She smiled. "Well, we won't keep you. It is a pleasure for me to meet you too." She shook his hand, hers cold and moist. She leaned toward him as she did so and said in a low voice. "He gets anxious sometimes after people visit."

He seems fine to me, thought Noah, but he didn't say anything, just nodded his head.

"Dinner is more than ready," said Angelica, motioning toward the dining room.

"Well," said Mr. King, "say goodbye to your friend, Brucie, and let's eat! I'm starved!" They headed off down the hallway, both looking back toward their son. He ignored them, opened the front door, and stepped outside with Noah.

"You'll need a coat out —" they heard Gwyneth King say, before she was cut off by the closing of the big front door.

"Oh, it is cold outside, colder than a witch's —" said Bruce, wrapping himself up in his own arms.

"You didn't need to come out."

"Your coat is awfully thin, Noah Greene."

"I have a warmer one at home. I'm fine, though. You had better get back inside."

"I wanted to thank you for coming over and talking to me, on a myriad of subjects."

"It was my pleasure. Can we do it again?"

"Again? You want to come over again?"

"On one condition."

"That I do not tell Miranda Owens?"

"Yes."

"I like that condition. I think I kind of love you now, Noah Greene." With that, he flung the door open and entered the house on the run, slamming the big entrance behind him with a smack.

Noah stood on the veranda in the cold for a long time just staring at the door.

When he got back onto the street, he didn't turn east to go home, but instead headed the other way toward Constance and Miranda's neighborhood. He knew Constance would likely be at dinner now, but he didn't care. Maybe it was a bit much to not text her before showing up on her doorstep again. It had been weird enough the first time. He took out his phone and found Constance's number.

Can I drop by to c u?

What?!

Just for a sec.

For what?!

Apologize.

For, like, yr life?

I'm here.

There was no response. Though that wasn't a "yes," it wasn't a "no chance" either. After he rang the bell on the Marks' front entrance, he heard another discussion, which quickly became an argument, about who should answer the door. The voices came from deep within the house. They were eating, as he had suspected.

The entrance jarred open. "You again?" said Mario,[55] who was obviously not pleased about having drawn the chore of getting the door more than once in two days.

"Yeah. Sorry about that. Can I speak with your sister, please?"

"She's eating."

"Sorry about that too, but it's important."

"I'll see what she says. She's a girl, remember that."

Mario closed the door on him and it didn't open again for a good two minutes. Noah could hear another discussion going on, this time between mother and daughter. When Constance came to the door, her mother was standing down the hallway, watching.

"Make it quick," said Constance.

"I want to apologize in person for the last time I was here. That was wrong. I get that. It was stupid."

"Okay. Goodbye." She started to close the door, but he pressed his hand up against it to keep it from shutting all the way.

"I would like to come back for another visit. On one condition."

"You are making the conditions? Look, dude, I haven't even said you could —"

"That you don't tell Miranda."

She narrowed her eyes and examined him.

---

55 Love this guy.

"Two conditions, actually," continued Noah. "The other is that you tell her what I did the first time, pretending to be a good guy, but really coming over to do something that would impress her. Tell her I haven't changed, that whatever it was that made me say that awful thing about her is still where I'm at."

Constance kept staring at him. "And," she finally said, "your reasons for wanting to drop by *here* in the future?"

"To talk. Really. Just to try to be friends."

"I'll think about it."

"Thank you."

She closed the door, a puzzled look on her face.

14

Better Me

NOAH STOPPED GOING TO the school weight room the next day. Instead, he started working out at home in his bedroom. They had two old dumbbells and one barbell with a rusty bar. He did some research online and set up a program for himself, one that wasn't calculated just to make his body look good, but was a healthy way to exercise too.

An uneventful Christmas came and went, during which he spent most of the holidays with his father, apart from a quick trip to Walker's house on Christmas Day at the insistence of his parents.

By the new year, he had a schedule for his exercising, weekly visits with Constance, Bruce, and Walker, and volunteer work helping newly arrived immigrants to read.[56] (He met the latter at the local Tim Hortons restaurant, where he knew Miranda never went.) Even with all that, he still managed to get in time for homework, basketball practice and games (during which he probably now passed the ball way too much), and, of course, a great deal of reading.

It took two weeks for Constance to allow him to stop by again and the first time he was there, she limited the visit to five minutes. Within a month, though, he was coming to the Marks' place regularly and he and Constance often talked so long that they lost track of time. They never once spoke of Miranda. He told her about his life and she told him about hers, and both were surprised to discover how little they really knew about each other. Constance, Noah discovered, was a caring and generous person, one who had had a terrible tragedy in her life that affected her outlook. He was shocked to hear himself telling her his innermost problems and fears, and at how good it made him feel to unearth them to this, in the end, actually non-judgmental girl.

Constance also mentioned Walker Jones often during their talks. Noah could tell that she liked Walk, from what she said, and that he seemed to like her too. It struck Noah that in a strange way, even though they were so different, they were perfect friends — one so outwardly sure of herself and decisive and the other unsure, but both of them insecure underneath. Constance wanted people to respect others. Both she and Walk

---

56 I know this all sounds like "goody-two-shoes" crap and sucky, but it's what I did. Sometimes people think they are too cool to be nice. I know I did.

craved respect. They were, in a way, two people in need of each other.

Bruce King turned out to be a good guy too, not just a strange little nerd whose personality you could put into a labeled box. Noah learned more about Bruce's rarely present, yet helicoptering mother and father under whose misguided parenting the boy was actually doing as well as he possibly could. Noah got Brew's conversation to slow down a little, and his need for fact-eruptions to lessen somewhat, and they came to like the times when they hung out together and said nothing. Noah even got Bruce to come out to play ball in Walker's driveway with the two of them and when Bruce hit his first long-range jumper, the celebration was something to behold.

And even though Noah kept crossing off the days on his calendar, and looking across the months to May 22, he stopped searching for Miranda every time he walked down the hallways at school. He didn't know if she noticed. He didn't care. Or at least, that was what he told himself.

He recorded it all in his novel. Every morning, before he did anything else, he sat at his desk and wrote for an hour. It was a strange thing: as he wrote, he knew there was something wrong with his conduct in the story, and not just in the early chapters. In some ways, there was something wrong with *why* he was writing it. He didn't want Miranda to know that he was truly trying to be a better person ... and yet he did. The novel itself betrayed his true feelings.[57] His whole life had become about May 22. What would she say? Would she be able to tell that he

---

57 That's what novels do, it seems to me.

had changed? Would his changes be enough? Would Miranda
Owens agree to go to the prom with Noah Greene?

The story, though, had a good arc. It had that interest in the
"what happens next" thing that it seemed to him was in all
good novels and it was moving toward an anticipated climax.
Any engaged reader would want to know what Miranda
Owens was going to say. It made Noah think about how life
was like a novel, or at least a play, like Shakespeare said. We
all play roles. All our lives have narrative, storylines. He wondered where in the world this narrative was leading him. He
wondered if his novel's conclusion would break his heart.

He kept reading the books Miranda had often talked about —
the ones that impressed her. He read them all the way through,
of course. He read all the novels in his Contemporary Literature course too, from cover to cover. The class was going to
look into *Infinite Jest* on February 25. He circled that day on
his calendar. He tried to read at least fifty pages of the big
novel every night. It continued to be confusing, funny, and
sad. It continued to have a massive number of characters in
what seemed to be a massive number of plot lines. Some of the
footnotes[58] were long, stretching over several pages. He kept
flipping back and forth from story to notes, working hard.

When he finally got to the end of the book, he had a strange
sensation. He wasn't sure what had happened. In fact, he was
sure that Wallace had written it so there was no ending at all
(since life was like that, at least while you were living it). If there
was an ending, it was one that Noah couldn't figure out. And

---

58 Though, again, they are technically endnotes … thought I'd use this foot-
note to note that.

yet, he loved it, and he knew, deep inside, what it was about ... though he couldn't articulate it. The best that he could come up with was that it was about life, about *now*, even though it was written quite a few years ago ... and it was about him.

WHEN FEBRUARY 25 ARRIVED, Noah was well prepared. The students had been asked to read as much of *Infinite Jest* as they could, fifty pages being the minimum. That got them into the story (or stories) a little and into a number of the endnotes. The first thing Mr. Mitchell asked them to do that day was be honest and indicate how far they had gotten. A couple of kids hadn't been able to ready fifty pages. Many had stopped at fifty. A few had been able to get past one hundred. And Miranda, of course, had read the entire book. Again. She said so without any undue pride, not in a quiet voice but not loud either. Noah knew that she had actually read it twice before this course even began — she had told him so on her veranda that beautiful night long ago — and had simply re-read it to refresh her mind this year. She could have easily told the class that.

When it came his time to say how much he had read, he said that he had not been able to get past the first page ... or at least that was what he had planned to say; what he actually heard himself declaring, almost involuntarily, as if his former self had momentarily possessed him, was that he had read it all. He said so in an attitude that was exactly like Miranda's. He tried not to slide his eyes in her direction as he spoke.

The discussion of what they had read went better. Noah let the others talk, even when he knew what they were saying was wrong. He simply interjected here and there to clarify what happened at certain points in the story. Miranda did the same, though she elaborated. In the end, Mr. Mitchell asked Miranda and Noah to stand up together in front of the class and tell the others what they thought of the novel. It was awkward. They stood there, girl and boy, their shoulders a foot apart. It was the closest he had been to her since they had broken up. Miranda never wore perfume, didn't believe in it, but she had a soap that she used, satsuma, and its fragrance, a sort of heavenly orange, had always made him feel wonderful. He stood beside her, that fragrance engulfing him: the scent of Miranda Owens.[59] He couldn't touch her, though, maybe never would again. It was like being within inches of everything you wanted but not being able to reach for it. He remembered there was a Greek myth about that.[60] The only good thing about this awkward moment from Noah's standpoint was that Miranda looked down at the floor too when she wasn't talking. It meant she felt something. What, exactly, he didn't know, but at least it was something, and that was amazing to him. Maybe May 22 was going to be a good day after all.

Miranda spoke well, of course, discussing the novel as a "prescient work of art written before the twenty-first century and yet predicting much of it" that tells "a good deal about modern western culture and about humanity itself." She gave examples. She said it was funny too, which both made her very happy and very sad. Then it was Noah's turn.

---

59 I hope that doesn't sound too weird, or creepy. It was what was really happening, though.
60 Couldn't find it.

It seemed like there was drop-dead silence for a long time after he was asked to speak. His heart was pounding. He wasn't sure, but it appeared to him that Miranda had slightly turned her head and was looking at him.

"It … it seems to me that Miranda is right," he said in a shaky voice. "I didn't really understand the book. It is very complicated." He went and sat down quickly, leaving her alone in front of the class. The most remarkable thing happened when he looked up at her from his desk: she was staring back at him. Their eyes met, truly met for more than an instant. For the first time in many months, there wasn't indifference in her expression and there wasn't hatred either.

His essay about *Infinite Jest* was a whole different story. He let loose. He unloaded everything he felt about the novel in the most insightful way he could. He talked about the use of footnotes (though he was careful to call them endnotes), how they broke up the regular way of telling a story and allowed the narrative to be different, made you think about stories themselves, made you work at reading the novel, literally work as you turned back and forth, instead of just being thoughtlessly entertained. He wrote of how the use of notes was also indicative of something that was going on throughout the novel — an imitation of the way the human mind works, with its myriad thoughts happening simultaneously, instead of the false idea in most novels that human beings always thought in simple, straight lines. He wrote of how the subtext was about many things, but mainly perhaps about our modern world of constant entertainment, its "prevalence" so "ubiquitous" that life had become entertainment. There were screens, phone-sized and larger everywhere, and apparently so-called "great" novels were just entertainment too these days. The film *Infinite Jest* in *Infinite Jest* drove that point home: the movie that entertained anyone who watched it so thoroughly that they were unable to do anything but keep watching it. He mentioned how today people spent *so* much time entertaining themselves. The novel, though, was also about the burgeoning mental illness all around us, our nearly endemic problem with anxiety, drugs of many kinds in our drug-filled world, the environment, and about politics and power. It also revealed how we are often so far from the truth about ourselves, how we have lost who we really are.

Mr. Mitchell let him know that he wanted to speak with him two days after the essays were handed in. Mitchell had given back all the others, except Noah's. Class was over. Miranda was the last person to leave the room. She didn't even glance back as she left.

"Have a seat," said Mr. Mitchell. He motioned to a desk. It just happened to be Miranda's. Noah sat down. He could feel her warmth, like a hug, and smell the Satsuma.

"Is there something wrong with my essay?" Noah blurted out.

"No. No, there's nothing wrong with it, to say the least. It is extraordinary. In fact, I am giving you 100 percent. I have never done that before for an English essay. I don't believe 100 percent is possible in the arts. You deserve this, though. You —"

"So, it's the top mark, higher than Miranda's?"

Mitchell smiled. "Yes, higher than Miranda Owens', though she wrote a wonderful piece too."

Noah couldn't stop a grin.[61]

Mitchell frowned. "That's not the reaction I was looking for."

Noah turned red. "Sorry," he said in a small voice.

"You know, Noah, you don't need to judge yourself by others or always try to impress ... I know about your situation at home, how you look after your father." He pointed to Noah's head. "There is a great deal to be admired inside there." He motioned toward Noah's chest. "And in there too. Remember that."

---

61 Yeah, I actually did that.

15

Penultimate

NOAH WORKED HARD ON his novel and on his conduct over the next three months. He wrote every night — thinking about the sort of story Miranda admired and trying to make his like that. He was motivated by the idea that she would be surprised at the ingenuity of this gift to her.[62] The character in the story truly loved Miranda Owens. In a way, it was an ode to her.

He decided to give the book to her the instant before he popped the question. He figured that might melt her, give him the best shot possible. He kept visiting Constance and Bruce (rarely Rosie, though). He maintained his commitment to the Tim Hortons meetings with the struggling readers, and he kept trying to be the best basketball teammate he could. He had

---

62 I'm actually worried that I haven't made the Miranda character flawed enough, since flawed characters are cool nowadays, and entertaining and needed in novels ... but the Miranda character is exactly true to life.

heard the great player Kawhi Leonard say, "I don't play hero basketball" and adopted that as his motto. He also tried to be the best and most modest student too. Before long, he had read every novel he thought Miranda admired, right through to the end.

BY THE TIME MAY 1 arrived though, he was focused on one thing: the scene in which he asked Miranda to the prom, both in real life and in the book. Where should he do it? How should he do it? How should he react if she said "yes" … or if she said "no"?

Spring was always the most beautiful time of the year in these parts, a re-birth of life after the cold winters — everything turned green, the flowers burst into bloom as if in celebration, and the air turned room-temperature perfect. It always felt like God or Mother Nature was smiling, glowing down upon the town. It was also, though, when pollen was everywhere, when some peoples' eyes turned red, their throats filled with phlegm, and they felt tired and unable to appreciate the re-awakening around them. Noah, however, did not have that problem. He didn't suffer from any allergies. Most years, he was one of the fish who was able to appreciate the water in which he swam.[63] That spring, though, he didn't. His thoughts remained full of Miranda, of what would happen on May 22.

THREE WEEKS BEFORE THE appointed day, however, his prospects seemed to dim. And the dimming happened with one glance at Miranda.

---

63 Worked hard on this part.

Though Noah tried to never so much as look her way at school, she seemed to walk around as if there were a light glowing down upon her. You couldn't ignore her. On May 2, that light became intense.

He was moving down the hallway with Walk.

"So, are you prepared for the *Hamlet* test?"

"Yeah, I guess so."

"What do you mean you guess so? We spent two hours on it yesterday."

"The most harrowing two hours of my life."

"Walk, you can do this."

Walker stopped in the middle of the hall and put his hand on Noah's shoulder.

"Yeah, I guess I can. And … thank you. I've never said that to you before, but thank you. Thanks for helping me, for being a good friend."

"That's okay, Walk. You're a piece of crap, you know, but you're a *friend* who is a piece of crap."

Noah expected that guy-thing comment to at least bring a smile to Walker's face, but his buddy didn't seem to be listening. He was looking over Noah's shoulder, staring, actually.

When Noah turned, he saw the spotlight, but it did not just feature Miranda Owens. There were two people in the light, standing close to each other at her locker. The other person was Andrew Chen. Nice, great-looking, intelligent, tall, dark-haired Andrew Chen, the same guy she had been riveted on at the basketball game, the same guy she had touched on his sweaty shoulder. She was touching him again, this time on the arm, caressing it,[64] running her soft long fingers along his hard forearm with its manly veins. She was looking into his eyes and he was looking back. They were both smiling.

A conversation he once had with Mir burst into his mind. For fun, one time, they had talked about their fantasy partners, allowing each other to choose simply based on looks.

"Be honest, Noah," she had said, snuggling up to him on her chesterfield, intertwined with him the way she always liked to be — there was a Dylan song about lovers being entwined that she adored[65] — her left leg crossed over his thighs, both her hands squeezing one of his, playing with his fingers. "Tell me, if you could have any girl in the world, appearance-wise, what would she look like?" She stared at him as she asked. He could see what he thought was hope in her eyes.

"Okay ... she would be short, heavy-set and dark, and have long hair."

She swatted him.

"Okay," he said. "I'll tell you the truth, God's honest truth." He stared back at her. "She would be tall; her nose perhaps a little long; have short, strawberry blond hair; and sparkling, pale blue eyes." He gazed at her, tried to look right into her. She believed him and it made those eyes water.

"How about you?" he asked.

"Honestly?"

"I thought that was what we were doing?"

"Okay." She paused for a moment. "I like the way you look.

---

64 Maybe that's a bit of an exaggeration.
65 Don't think I need to mention the title.

I love it ... I want it." He felt a warmth in his chest. "But ... if I were absolutely honest, I'm partial to the tall, dark, and handsome type too."

"What?"

"It's just a fantasy, Noah. You are my guy in real life."

ANDREW CHEN WAS PROBABLY six foot two. He had Noah by about an inch. He had coal black hair. He was looking down at Miranda now as she smiled back at him. He had never seen Miranda Owens interested in a guy, not outwardly, no guy other than himself. It took everything he had not to march over there and interrupt, to sock Andrew Chen right in the face. He was so entranced he didn't notice that someone had come up to him and Walk, and was standing close to them.

"Hi Rosie," said Walker. He sounded a little down, which Noah appreciated.

"Hi Walk ... Noah."

Walker turned Noah toward her.

"Haven't talked to you in a while. How are you doing?" she asked.

"I'm fine." He looked toward Andrew and Miranda again; he could not stop himself.

"He's cute," said Rosie as she looked toward the couple.

"Thanks for that scintillating piece of information," he snarled.

He left Rosie standing there, looking upset. He left Walk there too. As he marched out of the school, he noticed that Miranda moved over to them. At least she hadn't kissed Chen or anything. In fact, she actually seemed anxious to talk to Rosie.

IT WAS HARD TO return to his novel that evening. He didn't want to write the scene he had just experienced, and it wasn't only because of Miranda and Andrew, as painful as that was; it was also because of Rosie, of what he had said to her and how he had left her standing there, looking distraught. He knew that wasn't progress. He also knew how truly hard this thing he was trying to do really was.

THE FINAL THREE WEEKS seemed to go by in a rush. At times, he wondered why he was even bothering. Miranda would have a boatload of suitors for the prom, or at least, there would a pile of guys who would want to ask her. How many would have the guts was another question. That wouldn't matter though, nor would any of his efforts, if what he suspected about her and Andrew Chen was true.

Two days after he had seen them together, though, something unexpected happened.

He was with Walk again, moving down the hallway near where he had experienced that horrible scene.

Andrew Chen was near Miranda's locker again, but she wasn't there. In fact, as Noah neared, he realized, using his basketball peripheral vision, that he had just passed Miranda and she was standing across the hall expertly situated behind a few other students, watching what was transpiring near her locker, Constance Mark at her side, both of them looking excited. Rosie's locker was on one side of Miranda's and Constance's was on the other. Andrew was holding a girl's hand and looking into her eyes.

Rosie.

She was smiling at him, a big resplendent smile as wide as a hoop.

"Nice," said Walk into Noah's ear.

"What?"

"Looks like Rosie is getting her wish."

"Her what?"

"You're not telling me you didn't know that she likes A.C.? I'm guessing he just asked her to the prom. By the look of her, I'd say she said yes."

"I thought she liked —"

Walk smiled. "You?"

Noah was too embarrassed to respond.

"Yeah, she does. Of course she does, a lot, but she likes him too. You guys might be tied in her affections. She's an amazing girl, we both know that; she's allowed to like more than one guy and she deserves to be appreciated. She would have gone with you, for sure, but you know what they say: a bird in hand is ..."

His words faded as Noah glanced toward Miranda. She looked incredibly happy. It only then occurred to him that she had not been interested in Andrew Chen at all. She had been arranging things. It was amazing to look into her face and see her so happy and to know that it was so pure, totally created by the happiness of someone else.

Noah didn't know whether to smile or frown. It felt as if he had lost something, but gained something too.[66] As he looked at Miranda, so intrigued by her pleasure that he was

---

66 I know that's not a good way of putting it, but it's all I can think of.

actually staring at her, she glanced at him and her smile did not disappear.

He pivoted and caught back up to Walker Jones.

"Walk," he said, "has Miranda asked about me lately?"

"Haven't really —"

"I mean, does she notice the things I'm doing lately, the way I've changed?"

Walk gave him a bit of a look. "What are you doing lately?"

"You know."

"No, I don't. You're just being you, as far as I can tell."

He let Walk move on. He stood still in the crowd of students passing. They moved by like ghosts in a soundless dream.

"Maybe I should actually tell her that I'm friends with Constance, that I'm helping Bruce, that ..." He stopped those thoughts running through his head. He considered how her smile hadn't vanished when she'd noticed him staring at her. *She must know*, he thought. *Miranda Owens sees everything, even invisible things. She must know my spirit has changed.*

He went home later that day walking on air. It was May 20. Two days remained. This was getting real. It all seemed possible now: a happy ending to his story.

He went to the beach and sat on the sand where they had spread out their blankets almost a year ago, a Frisbee flip from the portable change rooms. The town employees had started putting them out again. He sat there and looked at the closest one. He wondered if that was the actual one where he had made his horrible mistake. He had not known a damn thing about girls, about how they should be treated, he knew that now.

He turned back and looked out at the still-cold water. It was time to make specific plans for his proposal. That was how he thought of it, as a "proposal."

Where should he do it? What was the right setting? Was there a place that might offer him the best chance of success? He thought of the beach, right here, but then dismissed that — he would have to somehow get her here and he knew he could not coerce her into going anywhere in particular. In fact, he shouldn't coerce her into anything, ever. He also thought that it might be too brave, too intimidating, to do it here anyway. The memories would be too painful for her. It would be interesting to say he was truly sorry and offer her his new self, his selfless self, his eternally changed self, right at the scene of the crime … perhaps, though, not a location for success.

"How about at school?"

"How about it?" a voice said.

Noah hadn't realized he'd been speaking out loud or that Walk had followed him to the beach from a distance and was now standing right behind him. Noah's head whipped around. "What the hell are you doing here?" he asked.

"Looking for my friend. You know that old 'a friend in need is a friend indeed' thing."

"You think I'm in need?"

"Yup."

"I'm guessing you have no idea why I'm —"

"You are thinking about Miranda. You are about to pop the question."

Now that Noah really looked at his friend, he realized that

he appeared unusually happy. He was grinning as he spoke and his face was flushed. When he sat down beside Noah, his leg was vibrating.

"What's up?"

"Oh nothing." Now his smile was wide, like the cat that swallowed the canary.

"Not nothing."

"Just, uh … got a date."

"To the prom?"

"Yes indeedy-do."

"Do I know her?"

"Oh, yeah."

"Who? Tell me, numb nuts."

"One Constance Mark."

"Constance? Really?"

"Yeah, great girl … great young woman. You know, Noah, all they really want is for us to treat them like human beings. If you do that, you've always got a shot. Great girl … young woman."

"You've already said that."

Walker leapt to his feet and started swiveling his hips. "R-E-S-P-E-C-T, find out what it means to me! Just a little bit … yeah!" He was belting it out.

"Okay, Aretha, that's enough."

Walk plopped down again. "You should have seen her when I asked her. I was nervous as crap, man —"

"That doesn't make any sense. Crap is not nervous. Bad simile."

"And she helped me. She smiled at me as I approached, as if she knew what I was going to ask her. It made me relax enough so I could get it out. She was awesome. She IS awesome. She didn't just say 'yes'; she said something like, 'of course, you doofus, what took you so long?' and it made me feel like a million bucks, like I wanted to jump over the moon or something. She made me feel like I really am somebody. Man, girls are magic, Noah. They have, like, magical powers."

"Tell me about it."

"Constance Mark and Walker Jones at the prom together! Constance Jones ... how does that sound?"

"Don't think she'd go for that."

"Yeah, you're right, and good for her. That's what I like about her. She's got, you know, balls."

"Let's set that image aside."

There was silence between them for a moment. All Noah could hear was the lapping of the waves. Walk had said girls simply wanted guys to treat them like human beings. Noah had been selfish, and especially when he said that horrible thing last summer. It was the default position for human beings, like David Foster Wallace said in *This Is Water*. Miranda wanted someone better and she had thought Noah was it. He'd proven her wrong.

"Sometimes you make a lot of sense for an idiot," said Noah.

"Thanks. Constance helps in that department. She taught me lots. Do you know about this thing called the Bechdel Test? It's a way to look at movies and books to see if they are fair to girls, or women. A story has to have at least one scene in it where girls, or women, talk to each other without a guy being in the scene, and talk about something other than guys, to pass the Bechdel Test. You know, I never thought about that sort of thing before."

There was another silence. Noah was thinking about his novel, wondering if he needed to go through it and get one of those scenes into it, right away. His story, though, was about a guy and a girl, inseparable, their lives entwined, everything in it involved both of them. His thoughts flew back to Miranda.

"So … it's my turn now," he said.

"Yup."

"Mine is the hardest."

"Bullshit. We all think that, and if we all think it then none of us are right."

"This is Miranda Owens, though, and after what I said about her and all our time together and —"

"Yeah, and mine was Constance Mark. Just as awesome, or more so, in my opinion, and I'd dug myself a big hole with her too."

"I'm doing it the day after tomorrow."

"Hope you aren't too late."

"What do you mean by that?"

"Nothing."

"What do you mean by that, knob-head?"

"Just rumors."

"What rumors?"

"I gotta go." His smile fell away a bit for the first time. "Good luck."

It was almost as if he were about to add — "you'll need it" — but he turned and walked away, leaving Noah sitting there, not far from the portable change room that had put him in the spot he was in now. He imagined what things would have been like if he had kept his mouth shut that day, if he had been a decent person, good to the girl he claimed he loved. They would have been the slam-dunk couple of the prom. He would have been beside himself with excitement and anticipation right now, not full of fear. Maybe they would have even taken their relationship a step further by now. Maybe she would have let him.

That struck him as a bad thought.

He got to his feet and walked off the beach. He moved slowly since he had so many things to turn over in his mind.

Before he was home, he knew where he was going to ask her.

16

What Happened Next

THE DAY BEFORE HE asked her was not a good day. It was crunch time when it came to asking girls — and guys — to the prom and there was a palpable tension in the school hallways. It felt like it was a do-or-die week. Girls seemed to be in charge: they were forming groups, online and off, to help other girls get invitations, working their connections, cajoling the guys they knew who didn't have dates. Guys were standing in front of mirrors at home, working on their asks ... or, with trembling fingers, pushing letters in carefully-worded texts, knowing that they were chickening out by taking that route. Girls were thinking of asking girls too, and a few guys were terrified about asking a guy.

Despite what Walker Jones had said, Noah believed that no one had the task that he had: asking Miranda Owens, and asking her when he knew that she had despised him for so long, and maybe still did.

He had twenty-four hours left. It was like being on death row.

Rumors were flying about and you could actually hear some of them if you listened carefully as you walked down the halls, or even sat at your desk, or paid attention between dribbles at basketball practice.

Noah listened carefully. It was mostly the girls doing the talking.

"So, Walker Jones is taking Constance Mark. Weird." He heard that more than once.

"Rosie Gonzalez got Andrew Chen. Can you believe that?"

"Noah Greene hasn't asked anybody. Somebody would say yes, wouldn't they?"

"He still wants Miranda."

"Good luck. She still hates his guts."

"Not what I heard."

He listened even more intently.

"Miranda ..."

"Miranda ..."

The sound of her name was like a magnet to his ears, even when he could not hear the rest that they said.

Then, sitting alone in the cafeteria, since Walk was over at Miranda's table with Constance, he heard everything said by a group of grade twelve girls — three of whom everyone considered the experts.[67] They talked as they worked their phones, and he heard it loud and clear.

---

67 Everyone knows whom I mean.

"Miranda has a suitor."

"Really?"

"In fact, she has at least two."

"Really?"

"One wrote a letter, an actual letter, and the other guy asked her in person."

"What did she say?"

"Spill the beans!"

"I hear she accepted one of the two."

The rest of their conversation didn't matter. Their words had pierced him through his heart. He didn't even care who it was.

He looked toward Miranda. She glanced back at him. She looked happy. Or maybe triumphant. He somehow got to his feet and trudged out of the cafeteria. He was thinking about going home even though it was still midday. He couldn't imagine facing any more classes.

In order to leave, though, he had to walk right past the girls he had overheard. They peeked up at him as he neared them and went quiet. Then, he swore he heard one of them whisper: "It isn't true." He stopped in his tracks. *It isn't true*. He looked back at them and picked out the one whom he thought had spoken. She lowered her head.

Had she really said that? He didn't know. He wasn't sure.

He went home.

HE COULDN'T EAT AND it took him a while to rouse himself from his bed and write more of his novel. He wrote about what had happened that day, not sure how to put it, how to structure it or phrase it. He wrote for a while and then got up and stood in front of the mirror, like so many other young guys were likely doing that night. He looked at Noah Greene who looked terrified.

Then he began practicing his speech. It didn't go well at first: a mumbled apology that did not sound sincere, followed by a profession of undying love that sounded staged and tears that most definitely weren't.

He stood in shock, wiping off his face, horrified that this might happen in person, right in front of Miranda. He started wondering if he could actually do this, and if she said "no," what in the world he would do.

He slapped himself, hard.

He tried again. This time, he picked up the manuscript for his novel and included it in his proposal. It went a little better. He looked into Noah Greene's eyes and spoke from the heart.

He did the proposal about five times. It continued to get better, but he wondered if it would be enough. He also wondered if the girls were right, at least what they'd said at first. Miranda had two offers. She had accepted one. He thought of her smiling face. Maybe there was no use in even trying.

He heard his father groan in the next room. He imagined his life going forward without Miranda Owens. He imagined becoming someone like his dad. The loss of his mother had destroyed his father.

He sat down at the desk again and with trembling hands, wrote the last chapter of the novel. He called it "What Happened Next." Really, though, it was actually the second-last chapter, the penultimate. Miranda, as he said in the introduction, would provide the ending.

What would that ending be?

"What would that ending be?"

The last word he wrote was *word*.

17
The Answer

NOAH HAD TO TIME it perfectly. He didn't go to school that last day. He, however, knew exactly when Miranda would arrive and when she would leave. She was disciplined. He knew a great deal about her schedule. He still did. If she didn't have basketball practice that day or one of her other commitments, she would step out of the school's doors at ten minutes after three. It would take her about fifteen minutes to walk home and she always walked. That meant she would approach the intersection about halfway between her house and Constance's at about twenty minutes after three. She would turn right there and walk to her place.

Other than making his father's breakfast and then making his own lunch at noon, he spent the whole day in his bedroom. With the noise from the television as his sound track — *Jeopardy*, sports highlights, *The Price Is Right*, a soap opera or two, *Jeopardy* — he went over and over how he was going to ask her. The proposal was now set into three parts. The first was the apology, the middle was about how he had changed, and the third was the ask. The one in the middle was the toughest. He didn't want to brag, in fact he didn't want to say anything about how he had become a better person, a person who would never say what he said before, a perfect man for her forever. He wanted Miranda somehow to know what he knew he should not tell her. He tried many different ways to express it and finally he decided to wing it. He figured he'd know what to do and say when the time came.

At two o'clock, he showered and dressed. He spent a good deal of time in front of the mirror, fixing his longish-brown hair. Miranda had said once or twice that she liked it best when it looked "disheveled," kind of messy. That presented him with a problem. How do you make your hair look perfectly messy? He worked on it for what seemed like close to an hour and it was getting late. He grabbed his novel, picked up the heavy winter coat she had given him (a key part of his plan), and raced out the door.

There were blue skies, just a wisp of cloud, and it was hot. He perspired as he moved quickly toward his destination, about half a block away from the intersection between Miranda's and Constance's places. When he arrived, he put on the heavy coat and stood there, breathing heavily, sweating so much that he could feel drips running down his forehead, likely messing with his messy hair. He clutched the novel to his chest.

She didn't come for the longest time. That worried him. A million thoughts ran through his head.

She is with the guy whose proposal she accepted. She changed her schedule because she wants to be different from the person she was in the past. She's been hurt, hit by a car, attacked by someone —

Miranda appeared. She was walking up the street toward him, her head down. Her manner of moving looked sad and contemplative. As she approached, she raised her head and saw him. He stood stock-still. From where he was, she looked puzzled for a moment. Then she started walking again, her eyes on him. As she got nearer, he started examining her expression at this closer distance. Did she look happy? Hopeful? Angry? Dismissive? It was difficult to tell.

When she reached the intersection, she turned and walked toward her house.

Perfect. He knew she would do that. It was part of his plan. It proved that they knew each other well. They were still connected.

He started to move. He turned at the intersection and followed her. They walked this way the entire distance to her house. Every now and then she would look over her shoulder almost as if, it appeared to him, she hoped he was still following. She seemed to be drawing him forward. A young woman drawing a young man to her. He was pretty sure she was thinking that too.

When she got to her house, she did exactly as he'd hoped. She walked up the steps to her veranda and sat down on one of the wicker chairs to watch what he did and to listen to what he was about to say. She sat there like his queen, waiting for his bow ... and his pitch.

He paused at the bottom of the three wooden steps. There were a million thoughts in his head. You had to write a long novel to capture the way a human being thought, and you needed footnotes or endnotes, a mile of them. You needed prose that was frantic and full of facts and anxieties and questions and everything.

I am standing here wearing her heavy coat. Does she get why I am doing that? Should the title of my book really be "The Book of Us"? Is that too much? It might help to get her to say yes. I need her to say yes. No, I don't. I should have made a cover for it before I gave it to her, made it look wonderful, romantic, maybe with a blue sky with clouds. Thank God I dedicated it to her. Did she receive a letter? Did another guy ask her in person? Did she accept? She is smiling. Or is that a smile? What does it mean? My default position is selfish, just like Wallace says, just like his was. I should have brought This Is Water *with me too, held it so she could see it. I need to tell her how I have changed. No, that is wrong. I need to speak in a calm, masculine voice. No, I need to sound anxious. I am anxious. I am sweating like crazy. She hates me. She loves me. She wants me to leave. She wants me to stay. Everybody worships. The only choice we get is what to worship. Do I worship her? Is that wrong? Do I worship what is right? Everything in our lives tells us that we are the center of the universe. We cannot deny that. We have to work with it, though.* This Is Water *says it is hardwired into us at birth. It says there is no experience we have ever had that we were not at the absolute center of. We need to understand that. We need to never crudely say that we had sex with the girl we love when it is not true simply to make ourselves feel better and impress others, at that girl's expense. We need to be better than that. She knew I had to be. I can try to adjust my natural default setting. Wallace tried. He failed. He was a human being. He tried again. He was a jerk. Like me. He knew he had to keep trying. He knew he had to at least tell us. He said we are the lords of our tiny, skull-sized kingdoms.* This Is Water *said we need to make the effort to truly care about other people and to sacrifice for others, over and over. It also said there are no atheists. Miranda knows all this. She knew it long ago. She knows that we always have a choice in life, a choice to read, to read purposely long, important books instead of entertaining ones, so we THINK, a choice to TRY to be a better person, a choice to be a better old man like Lear, to truly see others. ... I need to look after my father. He needs me. I must find more ways to help him. I am doing this, all of this today and for the last nine months, JUST to get Miranda Owens back. She is the PRIZE. I am still selfish. The novel is just to impress her. She is what I WIN for being a good person.*

THAT IS WRONG.

"Hi," she said.

"Hi," he answered.

It was the first thing they had said to each other since that horrible day on the beach.

"Do you want to ask me something?" She was smiling at him. *Really smiling.*

"Did someone write you a letter?"

"No."

"Did you answer any important questions lately? In the affirmative?"

She laughed. "No."

He took three steps up and stood on the veranda with her. They were in the same place they had been so many times before. Where they had sat at night in each other's arms, talking, and more. It was where she had given him the little book and told him to read it.

"Nice coat," she said.

"Thank you. Someone who cared for me gave it to me."

"Were those your only questions?"

"No, I have another one."

"Well ... ask me."

He looked right into her eyes and she looked back. Is it possible to know another human being or are we always foreign to each other? Even the people we love ... the people with whom we are *in* love.

He could not see the answer in her eyes.

I am only doing this to win her. I am still in my default position. This is wrong.

"Actually," he said, "I am out of questions."

"Oh?" She definitely looked disappointed. Her eyes appeared to moisten.

"All I want to say ... is that I am very sorry."

"Okay."

"And that I truly love you."

She looked back at him for a long time. "Is that everything?" she finally said.

"It's enough."

He turned his back on her and almost fell down the steps, clutching his novel, knowing now what the ending would be.

As he walked away, he kept waiting for her to call him back.

Acknowledgements

This novel began as an attempt to write a fictional story about the way boys interact with girls to whom they are attracted, and what they may or may not understand about them and how to treat them, at an age when they too are learning about relationships. I didn't want my boy to be a bad person, just a boy with boy tendencies and attendant faults. In other words, hopefully, real. I wanted to explore this issue from his perspective, something that, while not unique, does not seem to be common. I also wanted to see if I could write a story whose teenage characters were well-read and bookish, and still make it compelling and topical, and yes, in its own way, cool. At first, I thought that might be impossible. Then, I read John Green, an admirable author whose young characters think, read and speak as if they are as smart as adults. What a concept.

I want to thank my daughters Hadley and Johanna, who certainly played some sort of role in my wanting to write this novel. They are John Green fans and encouraged me to read him, and are certainly well-read themselves. They both read the manuscript with great care and commented at length about it, precipitating much (lively) debate between the three of us! They are two remarkable young women and their intelligent criticisms were invaluable.

I also want to thank Bronwyn Abreu, who as a student at Christ the King School in Calgary a few years ago, suggested the title (or something very near it) for *"The Book of Us"* when I invited her class to discuss possible titles for what was then an evolving story. I know she would have been friends with Miranda Owens!

Thanks as well to the team at DCB Books, my wonderful publisher, especially Barry Jowett and Sarah Jensen, who understood what this book was about and worked assiduously on it with me as allies in literature. Thanks too, to my agent Pamela Paul, always at my side in literary endeavors.

Shane Peacock is an author, playwright, journalist, and screen-writer, published in twenty languages in eighteen countries. He is a seven-time winner of the Junior Library Guild of America Selection, and twice winner of the Arthur Ellis Award. He has been shortlisted for the Governor General's Award, three times for the TD Canadian Children's Literature Award, and the Marilyn Baillie Picture Book Award. His picture book *The Artist and Me* was named to *Kirkus Reviews'* Best Books of 2016. His young adult novels include the acclaimed Boy Sherlock Holmes series, the Dylan Maples Adventures, and The Dark Missions of Edgar Brim trilogy. He lives in Cobourg, Ontario, with his wife, journalist Sophie Kneisel.

The author respectfully acknowledges that this novel was written while he was living on land located in the traditional and treaty territory of the Michi Saagiig (Mississauga) and Chippewa Nations, collectively known as the Williams Treaties First Nations, which include Curve Lake, Hiawatha, Alderville, Scugog Island, Rama, Beausoleil, and Georgina Islands First Nations.

We acknowledge the sacred land on which Cormorant Books operates. It has been a site of human activity for 15,000 years. This land is the territory of the Huron-Wendat and Petun First Nations, the Seneca, and most recently, the Mississaugas of the Credit River. The territory was the subject of the Dish With One Spoon Wampum Belt Covenant, an agreement between the Iroquois Confederacy and Confederacy of the Ojibway and allied nations to peaceably share and steward the resources around the Great Lakes. Today, the meeting place of Toronto is still home to many Indigenous people from across Turtle Island. We are grateful to have the opportunity to work in the community, on this territory.

We are also mindful of broken covenants and the need to strive to make right with all our relations.